"Talk about _____ heart-shape _____ would drive a saint to commit the unforgivable."

Aching for his kiss, Gaby reached for him at once. Luke closed his mouth over hers.

She knew this was a momentary aberration on his part. When he had satisfied the desire that had temporarily flared out of control, he'd let her go, regretting his weakness. They would return to their separate countries, separate lives. And that was the problem....

Over a century before, Gaby's great-grandmother had lost her heart to a sweet-talking, penniless artist and followed him to the ends of the earth— Las Vegas, Nevada. After meeting Luke, Gaby was beginning to know exactly how that felt. But where Luke went Gaby couldn't follow. She had no right to love him. The man she was holding on to she would have to let go. This moment would have to last her forever.

Dear Reader,

I find it absolutely amazing that it's the fortieth anniversary of the Harlequin Romance line. In fact, it gives me thrilling chills just to contemplate that that dates back to the year 1957!

You see—in 1957 my best friend and I, at the tender, impressionable age of seventeen, left the desert of Salt Lake City, Utah, to travel to Lausanne, Switzerland, *Heidi country*, where we attended a French-speaking boarding school with girls from around the world.

That was the year I was introduced to an entirely new world of people, languages, culture and travel. Little did I realize my mind was documenting every sight and sensation of that incredible experience for future use.

So 1957 was not only the red-letter year Harlequin started its bestselling Romance line, but the year the seeds of the writer in *me* were born.

Now it's 1997, forty years later. With thirty-seven plus books behind me, I find that it is indeed *a time to celebrate* with my latest book, *Second-Best Wife*, a passionate story of forbidden love that takes place in romantic Italy, the perfect European setting for this kind of intense tale. *Enjoy!*

Rebecca Winters

Second-Best Wife
Rebecca Winters

Harlequin Books

**TORONTO • NEW YORK • LONDON
AMSTERDAM • PARIS • SYDNEY • HAMBURG
STOCKHOLM • ATHENS • TOKYO • MILAN
MADRID • WARSAW • BUDAPEST • AUCKLAND**

If you purchased this book without a cover you should be aware
that this book is stolen property. It was reported as "unsold and
destroyed" to the publisher, and neither the author nor the
publisher has received any payment for this "stripped book."

ISBN 0-373-03460-1

SECOND-BEST WIFE

First North American Publication 1997.

Copyright © 1996 by Rebecca Winters.

All rights reserved. Except for use in any review, the reproduction or
utilization of this work in whole or in part in any form by any electronic,
mechanical or other means, now known or hereafter invented, including
xerography, photocopying and recording, or in any information storage
or retrieval system, is forbidden without the written permission of the
publisher, Harlequin Enterprises Limited, 225 Duncan Mill Road,
Don Mills, Ontario, Canada M3B 3K9.

All characters in this book have no existence outside the imagination of
the author and have no relation whatsoever to anyone bearing the same
name or names. They are not even distantly inspired by any individual
known or unknown to the author, and all incidents are pure invention.

This edition published by arrangement with Harlequin Books S.A.

® and TM are trademarks of the publisher. Trademarks indicated with
® are registered in the United States Patent and Trademark Office, the
Canadian Trade Marks Office and in other countries.

Printed in U.S.A.

CHAPTER ONE

"I'LL be with you in a moment, Giovanni!"

The rap on Gaby Holt's door was a prearranged signal she'd worked out with the polite, twenty-two-year-old Italian student who was employed at the ducal palace museum and spoke excellent English. They were the same age and had become good friends during her study-abroad program at the University of Urbino.

Lately he'd had a habit of coming by the *pensione* after her evening meal. They'd walk to the main piazza in the warm summer night, talk about Italian art and history, and eat *gelato*.

Gaby had fallen in love with Italian ice cream. She'd put on a few pounds since her arrival in Italy, which made her figure more voluptuous. In a few weeks, after she returned home to Las Vegas, Nevada, in the United States, she'd lose the extra weight naturally. With no more delicious Italian pasta, no cannelloni to eat, she'd probably starve to death.

Giovanni thought she was perfect just the way she was and told her to stop worrying. Gaby smiled. She'd fast learned that unlike American men, the Italian male loved women of all ages, shapes and sizes. Fortunately, Giovanni was the non-leering, well-mannered type. A sweet, entertaining companion who made her laugh and was a big tease, there was no sexual attraction between them to complicate their friendship.

If she had a problem with Giovanni, it was that he was only five feet nine inches, *her* exact height. Though he was strong and fit, she felt too big for him. To play down her appearance, she purposely wore flat leather sandals and kept her long, dark red hair confined in a braid.

One look at her reflection in the mirror and she decided a brocade vest over her cream-colored cotton top and matching slacks was needed to camouflage her curves. After rummaging through the mess on her bed, she found the desired garment and hurriedly put it on before opening the door.

"*Ciao*, Gaby."

"*Buona sera*, Giovanni," she answered in her best beginner's Italian. It was a beautiful language, but she had only learned the rudiments. *Oh, to have the money to stay here for a year or two and really learn it*! But at least she'd received a good start with her six-week language immersion program. Giovanni had been helping her learn her verbs. When she got back home, she'd take more Italian at the University of Nevada.

As they walked down the hall she stole a glance at him. Where did he get the suit he was wearing? He had no money. "You're all dressed up. How come?"

His warm, smiling brown eyes were the same color as his smooth cap of hair. "Since you will be leaving Urbino day after tomorrow, I thought I'd take you someplace special where they serve the best food in all Italy."

It sounded like he was planning to pay. She couldn't let him do that when he worked so hard for every lira. "I've already eaten, and I'm not dressed for anything special."

"You look perfect, and I know for a fact that you can always eat dessert."

She chuckled. "You're right about that."

"Then we will go. The *macchina* is parked behind the *pensione*."

She blinked. A *macchina* was a car. "I didn't know you had access to one."

They had reached the main floor of the boarding house where he ushered her past other students milling about until they arrived at the back entrance.

"Only on very special occasions. Tonight I thought we'd save ourselves some time by driving."

His reasoning made perfect sense. On this particular weekend, Urbino was swarming with tourists who'd come from all over Europe for a two-day Renaissance Fair. Held the last weekend of August, the beautiful mountain town in the Marches region, a two-hour drive north of Rome, had become a mecca for lovers of Renaissance history and tradition.

For Gaby, the fair represented the culmination of her studies in a country which had taken her heart by storm. The thought of going home to a boring desert of one hundred and five degree heat was killing her, but she had no choice. She'd run out of money and couldn't ask her parents for a loan when they were overextended financially as it was. Six children to feed and educate was no small task.

This had been her idea, her project. She'd earned the money for it. Meeting Giovanni had made the whole experience even more enriching, but it was fast coming to an end and she had to face up to her disappointment. Today her studies were completed. Tonight she determined to savor the activities and not think about leaving this paradise any sooner than she had to.

As they stepped out the back door, an elegant black sedan parked in the minuscule alley filled her vision. This was the first time Giovanni had ever provided them with any sort of transportation.

She turned to ask him what was going on when she saw motion out of the corner of her eye. Because of the angle of the auto, she hadn't realized that there was a chauffeur at the wheel.

In an economy of movement, the man in the driver's seat levered himself from the car. The moment passed in a flash, but it gave her enough time to sense that he was a powerful male, hard and lean, considerably taller than Giovanni.

The shadowy light prevented her from making out details, though she could tell he had black hair and was dressed in dark clothing.

"Gaby, allow me to present my elder brother, Luca Francesco della Provere, who is home from Rome for the festival."

His brother?

Gaby knew Giovanni had family, but she hadn't paid much attention because they were always so busy talking about their studies and interests.

Closer now, she could see a slight resemblance through the bone structure. But where there was softness in the angles of Giovanni's countenance, lines of experience had hardened his brother's aquiline features, and there was none of Giovanni's innocence in that brooding regard.

Those black eyes continued to appraise her, but his expression conveyed nothing of what he might be thinking. For an unknown reason, she shivered.

"You have a last name, *signorina*?" His deep voice revealed a less-marked Italian accent than Giovanni's. If his perfect English was anything to go by, he, too, appeared to have received the best kind of education.

"I—it's Holt," she stammered like a foolish schoolgirl. "How do you do?"

She would have put out her hand, but she had the oddest premonition that he wouldn't have reciprocated, so it remained at her side.

Gaby's European tour director, Gina, had warned her that because she was an attractive American on her own, she was a target for those Latin males who prowled for women with grotto-blue eyes and flawless creamy skin like Gaby's.

According to Gina, no Italian man could be trusted because they possessed an appeal and cunning all their own and represented danger to any woman whether she be nine or ninety-nine. Since they were master seducers, Gaby was to avoid them like the plague.

Gina had a rule of thumb. Never look any of her countrymen in the eye, never listen to their tragic, ridiculous stories meant to entrap you, always walk with a purpose. In most cases, the blatantly obvious, hopeful suitors would do nothing more than stare in adoration and eventually leave you alone.

At the Trevi fountain in Rome, where the local male inhabitants assembled in droves to watch the female tourists taking pictures of the statuary and then follow them around, Gina's advice had worked like a charm.

Gaby had managed to elude the most ardent admirers, specifically her Neapolitan bus driver who, though married with two children, flirted with Gaby every chance he got.

Oddly enough, the Provere brothers weren't anything like the men Gina had been talking about. Giovanni had never once come across as a man with a secret agenda. Nor had he pressed for a physical relationship with her. Initially, that was the reason why she'd allowed herself to become friendly with him at all.

As for his brother, who looked closer to thirty and was probably married, he didn't resemble the thousands of hot-blooded, working class, southern European males who conducted the local tours and waited tables.

On the contrary, there was an aloofness about him, an aura of wealth and refinement. The kind bred into his bones, which put him in an entirely different strata of man.

She was aware of an indolent ease in his demeanor which had probably been learned from the cradle because he'd been born privileged and cherished. Gaby had only had occasional glimpses of such men during early morning rush-hour traffic in the bustling cities of Rome and Florence.

They would alight from their Lamborghinis or Maseratis to enter their places of business. At the end of the day, she'd watch them whiz away into the twilight and wonder which palazzo they called home.

She could easily imagine this man returning to his fabulous family villa in Rome or, like several she'd glimpsed, hugging the mountainsides in this region of Italy.

If she were being fanciful, she could be forgiven. As Giovanni helped her inside the back seat of the plush automobile, which felt more like a dignitary's limousine, she noticed the ornament on the hood of the car which represented a crest of some kind with a coat of arms.

She couldn't imagine what it all meant and wanted to ask Giovanni. To her dismay, his brother had taken his place behind the wheel and started up the motor, which purred like an expensive German-made car. There would be no privacy now.

In any case, Giovanni had struck up a conversation with his enigmatic brother who drove to the end of the alley bordered by the bricked walls of centuries' old buildings. With several honks of the horn, he forced the holidaymakers to clear a path so the car could proceed.

While the latter made an occasional response, Giovanni, with his natural enthusiasm, did most of the talking. Except for a word here and there, the Italian flowed too fast for her to follow.

Giovanni acted happier than Gaby had seen him before. If the same dynamics applied in his family as in hers, the younger brother hero-worshipped the oldest one.

"Where are we going, Giovanni?"

She'd known him for six weeks, but this was the first time she had an uneasy feeling being in his company.

Except that Giovanni wasn't the one contributing to her distress.

The man studying her features through the rearview mirror was responsible for the trembling of her body. She'd become unbearably aware of him as a man, a brand new feeling for her. She didn't know how to begin to deal with it.

"Home," Giovanni answered, oblivious to the tension-fraught atmosphere in the car. "I've wanted you to meet my family for a long time."

"I'd like to meet them," came the automatic response, but she could scarcely concentrate. After being around so many olive-skinned, dark-haired European men, what mortified Gaby was to be caught staring at Giovanni's brother like she'd never seen the male gender before. So much for her tour guide's warning.

This wholly feminine reaction took Gaby by surprise. She averted her eyes and moved next to the door, away from his brother's line of vision.

"Where is home?" she asked in a quiet voice, hoping the other man couldn't hear her words.

In a surprise move, Giovanni shifted closer. "You know where I work," he whispered near her ear.

"Yes, of course."

"That's my home." He gave her cheek a kiss, then he sat back as they slowly made their way through the streets swarming with tourists.

Giovanni's behavior was totally foreign to her. Alarm bells went off in her head. *The ducal palace*?

"Be serious, Giovanni."

"I'm being very serious. Luca—" he called to his brother, giving the other man's broad shoulder a friendly squeeze. "Tell Gaby where I live. She does not seem to believe me."

"Stop teasing, please."

"What do you wish to know, *signorina*?" Giovanni's brother didn't sound as if he particularly cared one way or the other. "His home is at the palace, just as he said."

She stared at Giovanni in exasperation. This was no longer funny. "My brother enjoys a good joke once in a while. Is that what this is all about? A Renaissance custom? Like being at a masked ball, only you've decided to throw away your mask?"

Giovanni looked wounded. "On occasion I have been known to tease. But Luca never jokes about anything, do you, *fratello*?"

The word meant brother. Giovanni appeared to enjoy ribbing his elder sibling. Theirs was a strange relationship. She felt undercurrents but didn't understand them. Until the car stopped, she had no choice but to go along with their charade.

Her *pensione* was situated on the outskirts of Urbino. Slowly the car made its way into the center. In the off-season, it would have taken five minutes at most to reach the walled, ancient inner city. But due to the crowds out for the celebration, fifteen

minutes passed before Giovanni's brother was able
to maneuver them from the more modern area to
its Medieval heart.

Soon Gaby's attention fastened compulsively on
the rounded towers which formed the perimeters of
the ducal estate. The fading light of the hot summer
evening glinted from its recessed windows and
brought out the mellow pink rose color of its crenelated walls.

They didn't stop at a side entrance used by the
tour buses to gain entrance to the part housing the
museum. Gaby had known they wouldn't. The men
were playing a game.

She started to tell Giovanni that she hadn't fallen
for his trickery when the car unexpectedly turned
and followed a mazelike path. It led to an inner
courtyard of the castle and ultimately a covered
archway, taking her back to a time in the fifteenth
century when the awesome beauty of the
Renaissance camouflaged secrets, intrigue and
treachery.

"You are cold?" Their driver's low voice grated
on her nerves. He'd seen her body quiver in response to her surroundings and made no apology
for watching the two of them through the mirror.

Giovanni lifted her hand and kissed it. "You
don't feel cold to me," he murmured as they came
to a stop before an entrance portico.

A great medallion motif hung above the brass
door and the busts of Italian statesmen stood sheltered in the arched niches. But Gaby couldn't appreciate their splendor because Gina's rules about

avoiding Italian men had come back to haunt her with a vengeance.

She could have sworn that Giovanni didn't have amorous feelings for her, so why was he acting this way now? Was he just having some fun in front of his brother? At times Giovanni could be a terrible tease, like a couple of her brothers.

Each day when her classes were over, they'd laugh their way through their walks to galleries and old churches, anything free. "Tell me the truth. Are you two the sons of the chauffeur or the gardener? Is that how you got a job in the museum, how your brother drives this expensive car?"

His brown eyes danced before they flashed to the taciturn man at the wheel. "You hear that, Luca? She wants the truth. I have an idea. While I run in and inform Mama that we have company, you be the host and reassure my lovely guest."

"Giovanni—" she cried, and hurried to get out of the car to stop him. By the time she was on her feet, he'd disappeared. To her chagrin she'd been left alone with his brother, whose forbidding nature didn't quite mask his devastating sexuality.

Compelled by an urge she was helpless to fight, her vagrant blue eyes wandered over this imposing man who was Italian from the hand-sewn leather loafers cushioning his feet to the small gold cross nestled in the dusting of black hair on his chest.

When he breathed, she could see it glint through the neck opening of the black silk shirt where his skin appeared to be as darkly tanned as the rest of his hard-muscled body clothed in black trousers.

Unlike the other Italian men she'd met, however, her presence seemed to irritate him in some way. She almost felt as if he disliked her.

Most men, Italian or American, found her attractive to the point that they became obsessive about it. At times their unsolicited advances made her defensive.

She'd dated a few nice boys in college, and she adored her father and brothers. But it was a fact of life that she'd been fending off older men and unwanted admirers since she was fifteen years old. Giovanni's brother was proving the exception.

He made her feel that she'd trespassed on his private person. Otherwise his veiled black gaze wouldn't have returned the compliment by sweeping over her face and curves with a boldness she wasn't prepared for.

Gaby looked away, confused and shaken.

"Why pretend that you didn't know this was Giovanni's home, *signorina*?"

His question shocked her. Her gaze flew back to his. "You think I'm pretending?"

A long silence ensued. "My brother tells me you two met when you came to visit the palazzo museum."

"Yes, but he was a guide and—"

"He gave you a personal tour of the rooms housing the jewelry collection, did he not?" he broke in.

"Yes, but—"

"Then you know that the House of Provere has been in existence for over five hundred years."

Her arched brows drew into a delicate frown. Certain facts she'd been learning in her history class about Urbino came back to her. It was in this city that the Renaissance reached heights to rival Florence and Rome. During that period, there was a very important fourteenth-century pope who was of the lineage of Provere, endowing his family with riches beyond her comprehension.

A cry escaped her throat. "You don't mean that you and Giovanni descend from *that* Provere?"

He fingered his cross absently. "Your reaction almost convinces me that you know nothing of my little brother's responsibilities or his vast bank account."

"*What*?"

Confounded, her eyes searched the inky darkness of his for verification that he was telling the truth.

"You truly didn't know that he is the most important person in Urbino?"

Incredulous, she cried, "*Giovanni*?"

Her thoughts darted back to the pleasant, studious young man with whom she'd been spending her free time. She'd assumed he was as poor as she was. He walked everywhere and never spent money except to buy them a drink. Often she insisted they go Dutch treat, and he went along with it.

Through new eyes she surveyed the castle walls, the grounds and enclosed garden filled with topiary trees and flowering bushes of every hue. She tried to picture Giovanni as master of this ambience, and couldn't.

The only person she could imagine fitting such a role was the disturbingly masculine figure trapping her between the car and the entryway.

Their gazes held until she could hardly breathe from the tension stretching between them.

"When our mother dies, he'll inherit the title of Duke."

A hand went to her throat. "Your mother is titled?"

Another troubling silence enveloped them. "Though titles aren't used today, our mother is the veritable Duchess of the House of Provere."

She shook her head. "I had no idea. He's only ever said that he had a family, but he's never talked about anyone in particular. I—I know nothing about you." Her voice throbbed.

A tiny nerve throbbed at the corner of his sensual mouth. Her oldest brother, Wayne, had a similar tick that only showed when his emotions were in upheaval.

"One day Giovanni's word will be virtual law. He'll command the respect of everyone in the Marches province. So will his wife," he added in a grating tone.

"Why do you suppose Giovanni has been so secretive?" Her voice pled with him.

His answer was a long time in coming. "Every man wants to believe that the woman he has chosen for his bride loves him for himself, and no other reason."

"*His bride*?"

Luke's lean body tautened. "Surely by now you must have guessed that our mother is inside the palazzo waiting to be introduced to the *future* Duchess of Provere.''

When his words finally computed, she groaned aloud, unable to take it in. "Tell me you're not serious.''

His dark brows furrowed. "I assure you I would never lie about something as crucial as my brother's happiness.''

"But I'm not in love with Giovanni,'' she replied in complete honesty before she broke down and buried her face in her hands.

"He hasn't asked you to marry him? The truth now!'' came the sharp demand.

Her head flew back, revealing tear-stained cheeks. "No! The subject has never come up. He's a dear friend, but that's all.''

A grimace marred his dark features. "Then he must be the last person to know it. It appears you've captured his heart, something no other woman has been able to accomplish,'' he murmured in thick tones.

"Did Giovanni *tell* you we were getting married?''

His eyes wandered over her upturned face. "He has gone so far as to assemble the family to meet you, which is virtually the same thing. He phoned me in Rome, insistent that I come home for the occasion even though he knew that I had—'' He paused. "Well, let's just say I had other pressing commitments.''

Though the night breeze was warm, she shivered. "I can't imagine what he's thinking. Even if I were in love with him, I'm totally unsuitable and he must know it.''

Giovanni had been born into a royal house linked to the papacy, had been brought up in these incredible surroundings, enjoying luxuries most people couldn't even imagine.

Their family name was held in the highest repute, one of the greatest houses of Italy. Their family crest was emblazoned on the pages of the country's textbooks, not to mention their fleet of cars.

If she were in Luke's place, she'd be more than skeptical about his brother bringing home a foreigner to meet the family. No wonder she'd felt that hint of animosity.

She was from America, that upstart nation from across the Atlantic, as the Europeans viewed it. A penniless college student who was still having trouble pronouncing *Prego* correctly. The only girl among five brothers sadly lacking in the polish and education of a woman fit to be Giovanni's wife and chatelaine of such a dynasty.

Clasping her hands to keep them from shaking, she asked, ''Do you think you could find Giovanni and tell him I have to talk to him right away?''

Before his eyes narrowed, she saw anguish in those black depths.

''I love Giovanni more than my own life, *signorina*. Under the circumstances, I'm going to insist that you allow him to keep his fantasy until after dinner when you are alone with him. I refuse to see him destroyed before the festivities begin.''

''But that would be dishonest to everyone!''

"No more than he has been with you," came the retort.

She shook her head. "I couldn't do that to your mother. It wouldn't be fair."

"Our mother will survive. It's Giovanni I'm concerned about," he said in bleak tones.

"Luke?" she called to him without thinking. His head reared back as if she'd struck him. *"Signore*—" she amended, embarrassed for the faux pas, "I'm sor—"

"It is not necessary to apologize," he interjected on a terse note. "I'm not used to hearing my first name pronounced in that way. What were you going to ask me?"

For a moment Gaby couldn't think. Heavy perfume from the roses filled the night air, making her senses swim. Luke had been talking to her about his brother. Yet her mind couldn't concentrate on anything but the virile man standing in front of her. In his presence, new inexplicable yearnings were coming to life.

A soft breeze had sprung up, disturbing his luxuriant black hair. It overlapped his tanned forehead. There were stray tendrils at the base of his bronzed neck, as well. She wondered what they would feel like if she touched them, touched him...

"Signorina?" he prompted.

Gaby was thankful for the darkness. Otherwise he would have seen the blood rush to her face.

"It's possible you've misunderstood Giovanni's actions. Maybe he got tired of the responsibility, he decided to play the pauper and give the prince a rest."

When Luke didn't say anything she started talking faster. "I—I'm sure this was part of his plan for the Renaissance Fair— To spring a surprise on me by visiting the ruling family of the province, a family who just happens to be his own flesh and blood. With his sense of fun, it's the kind of thing Giovanni would do, don't you think?"

Still he said nothing, only watched her mouth with unnerving intensity.

"If he wanted me for his wife, I would have known about it long before now, and then none of this w—"

Luke's grim countenance choked off the rest of her words. "Giovanni wants my consent before he marries you. It's the only reason I came home. As it is, I must return to Rome in the morning."

"*You're leaving so soon?*" she blurted, her disappointment more acute than she would have believed.

Luke's chest heaved, revealing its definition through the thin silk material, making her more aware of him than ever. Her mouth had gone so dry it hurt to swallow.

"Poor Giovanni. He won't want you to go. I can tell he loves you very much. I have a feeling he always listens to you."

He stood closer to her now. She could feel the shudder that passed through his taut physique. "Yes," came the haunted reply.

"Then before it's too late, go inside and tell him you don't approve of me, which is only the truth. Please, Luke—" she appealed to him in an agonized whisper.

"Per Dio." The muttered imprecation sounded torn out of him. "What you are asking of me is impossible. No, *signorina*. Giovanni has made his plans. I won't shatter his dreams and turn the occasion into a nightmare. *Neither will you,*" he warned in a voice of unquestioned authority. "It appears we are both doomed to play a part until he takes you home."

Much as she hated to admit it, Luke was right. She could never hurt Giovanni intentionally. But she didn't know how she was going to make it through this dinner, let alone confront him later.

"My brother is without guile," he murmured thickly. "That is why everyone loves him and would never want to cause him pain. When he phoned to tell me about the American girl I must meet, there was such joy in his voice, I couldn't bear to disillusion him until after I'd met you in person."

Her instincts hadn't been wrong. "I knew you disliked me." How she hated the tremor in her voice. It couldn't help but let him know the depth of her hurt.

There was a sharp intake of breath. "Not you, *signorina*. The *idea* of you. I've never felt that any woman was good enough for my brother. Ironically, I now find that I must revise that opinion."

His admission was the last thing she would have expected to hear. It filled her with wonder.

"If this were several hundred years ago, I would ignore your feelings and force you to marry my brother to give him his ultimate happiness."

She raised startled blue eyes to him. "You mean, if you had been duke, your word would have been law. How is it that Giovanni is going to inherit the title when *you're* the firstborn son? I don't understand."

Even though night had fallen, she could see his expression close. With a new sense of loss she watched him retreat to that inner part of himself where he was impregnable. The intimacy they'd shared for those few, brief minutes was gone.

Devastated, she said, "I'm sorry. I didn't mean to pry."

"You wouldn't be human if you didn't ask. Unfortunately, now is not the time to discuss it. Giovanni will be looking for us and I haven't yet fulfilled my duties as host."

When he started toward the entry, she hung back. He paused on the step, a magnificent figure in black. Perspiration broke out on her brow. "I'm frightened, Luke."

He raked through his hair. "Then you're not alone," came another of his shocking confessions. "I'll meet you inside."

CHAPTER TWO

SOMEWHERE in the huge palazzo Giovanni was talking to his family, but the enormous rooms swallowed sound. Like wandering into a church when no one was about, Gaby had that same isolated feeling now.

Luke had given her a moment alone to compose herself. He must have needed some time to himself, as well, but she wished he were here so she wouldn't feel like an intruder.

Her misgivings slowly changed to awe however as she found herself surveying the gallerylike foyer that had been part of Luke's home since birth. Above her head, the fantastic frescoes on the vaulted ceiling represented an allegory of the triumph of spiritual love. Gracing the walls were important scenes of the Provere family history.

Through one set of double doors she saw into another room devoted to the sun-god, Apollo. Over the head of the twenty-foot-high statue dominating its center, she grew dizzy studying the frescoes depicting one of the most famous legendary Greek myths.

Dazzled by the palazzo's priceless artwork and treasures, she moved to a sitting room containing trompe l'oeil panels with eighteenth-century Gobelin tapestries and Savonnerie rugs. Like a sleepwalker, she moved from room to room until she came to one which she claimed for her favorite.

Square in shape rather than rectangular, the floor gleamed of pure white marble. Every wall-covering, the richly hued draperies, the antique porcelain urns filled with fresh cut flowers, the Louis XV furniture and bracket clock, the frescoed ceiling with its depiction of heavenly angels surrounding God, all were a blend of red and white.

So exquisite was the harmony of design and color, so charming were the various appointments of the room, she had difficulty believing this was the work of human hands. If her eyes didn't deceive her, the central medallion over the doors was the work of one of the great Italian masters.

"Like you, my mother prefers this room to the others, *signorina*."

The deep, vibrant voice brought a surprised gasp to her throat. She whirled around to face the charismatic man responsible for the rhythmic change of her heart. *He'd been following her.*

Propped negligently against the door, his hands in his pockets, he murmured, "My father called her his *testarossa*. Perhaps there's a correlation."

"I don't know what that word means."

"She has red hair, too."

His hooded gaze took in her braid and everything else in between until it reached her sandals. Such a frank appraisal couldn't have been any different than the one she'd given him by the car. But now her palms grew moist and her body ached with inexplicable longings she'd never had to combat before.

"If I had known all this was Giovanni's heritage, I would have begged him to bring me here much sooner. I can't claim to have seen very many palaces, but this must be the most gracious, glorious home in Italy, if not Europe."

He gave a barely perceptible nod of his dark head. "Let's say it's one of the few."

"Am I right in thinking the medallion is Michelangelo's creation?" She must look such an anachronism against the bygone splendors of this room.

"You are," he murmured at last. Hearing his voice made her realize he was answering her last question rather than her own tortured thoughts.

"Cardinal Alessandro commissioned Francesco Salviati to create the gallery frescoes. Cardinal Odoardo employed the genius of the Carracci brothers who were responsible for the frescoes in the rest of the rooms.

"Many of the drawings are by Lagrenee, the statuary by Glycon. The palace architecture itself is the work of Sangallo, Giacomo della Porta, Vignola, and Michelangelo, not necessarily in that order."

Some of the most illustrious names in Italian art history. No wonder Giovanni was such a fountain of knowledge on the subject.

"Do you have any other questions?"

She wrung her hands. "Dozens, actually, but I can't think of one when I know I'm going to be meeting your mother in a few minutes. Is she happy for Giovanni?"

A mask slipped into place, wiping any expression from his arresting features. With negligent grace, he pulled away from the door. "Giovanni is the child she almost lost in childbirth. The son she worships."

What about you, Luke? Doesn't she worship you, too? The questions reverberated in her heart for no good reason.

"For the last six weeks our mother has known that she isn't the only woman in his life anymore. I'm afraid she's not ready to give him up without a struggle."

Gaby rubbed her aching temples. "But she isn't going to have to give him up! Before dinner starts you could take her aside and tell her everyth—"

"Brother Luca—" Giovanni suddenly appeared in the doorway, effectively terminating a conversation which was tying her in knots. "What terrible family secrets have you been telling Gaby to produce that look on her face? Come. Mama wants to meet you."

Gaby's eyes implored Luke, but he remained an implacable figure. Her gaze flicked back to Giovanni. "I wish you could have warned me what was going to happen tonight."

He smiled, ignoring her distress when he knew full well that she was overwhelmed by everything that had transpired.

"Then you wouldn't have come. Admit it. We're not such an awful bunch as Luca has made us out to be. No poisonings have been reported for at least two years. Isn't that true, *fratello*?"

Normally she would have laughed at his remark. He could be very funny. But this was no laughing matter. She refused to look at him or his brother.

"If you wish, I will ask everyone to remove their rings before dinner."

"Giovanni—" she cried in exasperation. He had no idea how she was suffering inside. His was the sin of omission, but a sin all the same.

Praying he wouldn't announce something patently untrue which would rebound on all of them before she could escape the castle, she reluctantly accompanied him through the palatial rooms.

Luke might not be in her line of vision, but the prickling of hairs on the back of her neck let her know he wasn't far behind. She brushed one hand against her hip in a nervous gesture, wishing she hadn't worn pants. Though perfectly modest, they revealed too much of her figure to a man who made her feel her femininity to the very core of her being.

Breathless before they reached the grand salon with its walls of sage green damask, she counted twenty-six smartly dressed adults of all ages assembled. They sat in groupings near an antique piano at the end of the oblong room.

Beneath one of four magnificent chandeliers suspended from the painted ceiling, Gaby picked out Signora Provere. Small in stature like Giovanni, her short, stylishly cut Titian hair made her stand out from the others. For a woman in her sixties, she looked younger and perfectly lovely in a hyacinth-toned silk dress.

Gaby had difficulty believing this woman had given birth to Luke until she left off talking to one of the relatives and trained dark brown eyes on Gaby.

There was no question that her piercing regard hinting at an indomitable will, plus the possession of a daunting hauteur, had been passed on to her firstborn son.

Luke's father must have been responsible for the black hair and tall bone structure which had gone to create the most striking male she'd ever known or imagined. If there was a strong physical resemblance to his father, then Gaby had compassion for Signora Provere's loss because there was no man to compare to him anywhere.

"*Mama? Vorrei presentare la Signorina Holt.*"

The older woman lifted one hand to her younger son for him to kiss, the other for Gaby. "*Piacere, signorina.*"

Giovanni's mother used the word "delighted" in her response, but the cool, very brief handshake and lack of facial expression denoted not only extreme reserve, but distaste. If the situation had been different and Gaby had been hoping to become Giovanni's wife, she would have been crushed to tears by his mother's cold reception.

"*Piacere di fare la Sua conoscenza, signora,*" Gaby replied in her best Italian.

The older woman shook her head and gazed at Giovanni, perplexed. "*Mi dispiace, ma non capisco.*"

Gaby knew her Italian pronunciation wasn't perfect, but unless Giovanni's mother was hard of hearing, she couldn't have misunderstood her.

"I have no problem with her Italian, Mama."
Giovanni championed Gaby, yet he showed no sign
of irritation toward his mother. "With your permission, I will introduce her to the rest of the
family."

Not waiting for a nod of approval from his
parent, Giovanni began the lengthy process, which
turned out to be an even greater ordeal than Gaby
had expected.

Not because he'd said something he shouldn't.
To her relief, and undoubtedly to Luke's, Giovanni
explained that Gaby was a close personal friend and
left it at that. Except for an aunt on his mother's
side, and a pretty young woman close to Gaby's
age who'd been presented as a goddaughter, the rest
of Giovanni's relatives were enthusiastic in their
greetings and made her feel welcome.

They seemed as sincere and cordial as any group
of people might be when meeting a stranger. As for
Luke, he remained in the background. A dark, un-
smiling figure, he stood near a lighted candelabra
which was as tall as he was.

Several times Gaby's gaze unexpectedly met his
and she'd quickly look away again, wondering what
he was thinking behind his relentless scrutiny. If he
had a wife and family, a possibility which was becoming more and more insupportable to Gaby, then
they weren't present, nor was there any mention of
them.

While Giovanni related anecdotes that made
everyone laugh, Gaby only went through the mo-
tions of responding. It was like being in a strange
dream, with Luke her one reality.

"*Giovanni, mio figlio*," his mother called to him. "You will accompany me to the dining room. Luca will help Signorina Holt to her seat."

Giovanni chose that moment to take her hand and kiss it. "You're trembling," he whispered against her hot cheek. "Do not be afraid of my brother. I'd trust him with my life."

Gaby could understand Giovanni's devotion. Luke had a natural presence that inspired confidence as well as other more disturbing emotions she didn't dare admit to feeling. Giovanni must never learn of her attraction to his brother.

"Enjoy your dinner," he continued to murmur. "I asked the cook to change tonight's menu. He has prepared all your favorite dishes."

She felt like laughing hysterically. Giovanni's behavior left no doubt in anyone's mind that he was a young man in love. Worse, his reference to the dinner specially prepared in her honor was guaranteed to alienate his mother.

Gaby would choke on food right now. Luke must have sensed her traumatic state. Her heart thudded at his approach. "*La nostra madre* is waiting," he said in an aside to his brother.

For once, Giovanni's eyes did not smile at Luke. "Take good care of Gaby. She's a little fearful of all of us."

After he let go of her hand, he walked across the salon to escort his mother to the dining room. Gaby had no choice but to wait for Luke who seemed disinclined to follow the others out of the room.

"A word of warning, *signorina*. The seating arrangements have been prearranged. You will be placed between me and Efresina Ceccarelli. Until you appeared on the scene disrupting our mother's carefully laid plans, Efresina had every hope of becoming the next duchess.''

Gaby thought back to the pretty young woman with fine brown hair who had snubbed her during the introductions.

''Just so you know, Efresina has loved Giovanni from childhood, so be kind to her.''

''As if I wouldn't—'' Gaby's voice shook with pain and indignation. She started to turn away from him when a hand of steel closed around her wrist, holding her in place.

Her startled gaze flew to his dark, intelligent face. It was the first time he'd touched her. She wished he hadn't.

The sensation of skin on skin drove all coherent thought from her mind, leaving her body an aching mass of nerves, of wanting for things she shouldn't be entertaining under any circumstances.

She must have communicated something of what she was feeling because he suddenly let go of her arm, as if her skin had burned him alive.

''I only said that because you can afford to be gracious. You're the one Giovanni wants, and no other. He made it undeniably clear when he asked me to safeguard you a moment ago.''

But I don't want him, Gaby moaned inwardly. She'd never truly known the meaning of the word want. But just being in Luke's presence had awakened something in her which she sensed could burst out of control given the opportunity.

Afraid he would devine her feelings, she tore her eyes from his face. She couldn't just stand there, and finally hurried past the piano to gain the next room. But her footsteps came to a standstill when she realized she'd entered the dining room where everyone's eyes registered surprise at her precipitous entry.

She could see two empty places at the end of the banquet-size dining table and headed in that direction. Giovanni and his mother sat at the opposite end.

Luke appeared at her side to pull out one of the Queen Anne-styled chairs so she could be seated. The grandeur of the room was illuminated by a groin-vaulted ceiling frescoed in the *quadratura* style, but Gaby couldn't appreciate it, or the lavish appointments of the dining table.

The ornate gold candelabras, crystal, silver and hand-painted china, all displaying the family crest, had little impact because her awareness of the disturbing male at her side had rendered her witless. It was impossible to concentrate on anything else.

She turned in Efresina's direction to make an effort at polite conversation, then gasped because she found herself staring into a pair of familiar, piercing black eyes beyond the other woman's shoulder.

They belonged to the tall, magnificent, white-robed figure depicted in the huge oil painting dominating the room. Without the mitre and other accoutrements of his holy office, the famous fourteenth-century pope of Provere lineage could be Luke incarnate.

His imposing stature, the strength in the jawline, the shape of the straight nose, the width of shoulder, the midnight hair, all his superb male attributes had been handed down through the genes to live five hundred years later in Giovanni's brother. Except for the fact that Luke wore black, the two could be twins. Incredible.

"Signorina Holt has already noted the strong resemblance between me and my illustrious ancestor." Luke spoke to the woman at Gaby's other side. "Since my mother insists on keeping the painting in here, rather than the museum, it would be impossible not to notice it, isn't that true, Effie?"

The woman warmed to his use of her nickname, but Gaby was still reacting to the uncanny likeness of the two men.

"Surely the public could never appreciate it the way we've done over the years, Luca."

After a small pause, she faced Gaby. "Do you have any idea of his importance in Urbino's history, *signorina*?" Her brittle question asked in excellent English warned Gaby to tread carefully.

"I've learned something about his prominence in my classes here at the university, Signorina Ceccarelli."

"Oh, yes. You're a foreign student. Why did you come here to study? Le March is not well known abroad. Most Americans flock to Florence or Sienna." She said her words loud enough that she'd caught the attention of everyone at the table.

Silence reigned as Gaby lifted her wineglass and took a sip, hoping it would help fortify her for the onslaught ahead. Apparently Giovanni had not told his relatives anything about her.

"My great-grandmother used to say the same thing. She lived to be ninety-nine. Before she died, I had to promise her that when I grew up, I would go visit her birthplace."

"Your great-grandmother was Italian?" Efresina's shock seemed as profound as Signora Provere's.

"Yes. She was born Gabriella Trussardi, from Loretello. I was given her name because I inherited her red hair."

Immediately there was an explosion of excitement around the table. His mother looked as if she'd gone into shock, but Giovanni smiled at Gaby across the expanse. He seemed to have a penchant for doing the unexpected and was enjoying the little bomb she'd dropped on his family.

"Your connection to Marchigiani blood, as well as your red hair, has taken our mother by complete surprise," Luke muttered in thick tones.

"But surely Giovanni told you."

"My brother laughs and teases to cover up his emotions. The truth is, his innermost thoughts run very deep and no one is privy to them unless he chooses otherwise."

As far as Gaby was concerned, Luke wasn't that different from his brother. Did anyone have access to his soul?

Just then another relative sat forward and addressed her. "What did your great-grandmother's people do, *signorina*?"

The man at her side was waiting, listening. It robbed her of breath. "From what I understand, they were poor farmers."

Another blow for Giovanni's mother to sustain, but he had placed Gaby in this untenable situation. She couldn't be rude and not answer their questions, even if the answers were unpalatable.

"Tell us more."

Gaby tortured the end of the napkin lying across her lap. "She fell in love and ran off with an impoverished artist from New York who would give away his paintings in exchange for board and room during his travels. They got married somewhere in Europe, living hand-to-mouth.

"Before World War Two broke out, my grandmother was born. At that point he decided to take his family back to the States, to the West where his artist's eye became enamored with the desert. They ended up in Nevada, my home."

As if coming to her relief, the uniformed servants began bringing food to the table, suspending conversation until everyone was served.

Through veiled eyes Gaby watched Giovanni's mother receive her second shock of the night. Instead of five courses, the entire meal had been put on one plate. All Gaby's favorite foods—buttered *tagliatelle*—noodles—veal cannelloni, a rich flatbread known as *crescia*, and peach *gelato* in a crystal dessert bowl. Hers had two large scoops, drawing everyone's attention.

While Gaby blushed, Signora Provere spoke in rapid Italian to her younger son, most likely telling him that nothing like this had ever been done before. His mother was being put through needless torture. Gaby groaned in pain. Food was anathema to her right now.

"Giovanni has risked our mother's displeasure by countermanding her orders to the cook. You can't refuse to eat when he has gone to so much trouble for you."

"I won't," she whispered, knowing what she must do without his prompting. Though she might have to run to the bathroom later, she would do justice to her meal.

Everyone did the polite thing and carried on with the dinner as if nothing untoward had happened, but Gaby noticed that the dainty Efresina only toyed with her food. Luke didn't bother to make a pretense of eating. But Giovanni wasn't watching him.

Being a taller woman with a fuller figure than the other females present, Gaby felt like a glutton eating everything including her last spoonful of ice cream.

"How did you like your dinner, Gaby?" Giovanni's voice spoke to her across the long expanse.

She took a deep breath. "It was wonderful. You were right. This is the best food in all Italy. Thank you for being the perfect host, Giovanni."

His face broke out in a broad smile. "More *gelato*?" He had done everything in his power to please her.

She was on the verge of being sick, but didn't want to disappoint him. Out of the corner of her eye she saw Luke's full plate and it prompted her to say, "If I want more, I'll finish your brother's."

The moment the words were out, Luke's hand tightened into a fist on his hard-muscled thigh.

Giovanni grinned, oblivious to the undercurrents. "Normally Luca loves sweets, just like you. Since living in Rome he probably doesn't get them as often, and is a little out of the habit. Isn't that true, *fratello*?"

CHAPTER THREE

As IN the car on the drive to the castle, Giovanni enjoyed teasing Luke. She presumed it was because he missed his brother so much, this was his way of showing affection. But at the same time it created a strange kind of tension in Luke. She could tell it disturbed him on some elemental level not easily discernible to the others.

"Have you had an opportunity to visit Loretello yet, Signorina Holt?" one of Giovanni's uncles addressed her. His question didn't allow her to dwell long on Luke's private torment, whatever it might be.

"Yes. I went a few days after my arrival in Urbino. Before her death, my great-grandmother described it to me, but nothing I'd pictured in my mind prepared me for my first look at that tiny, fortified town."

He smiled. "You like Italy?"

"I love it so much that when I get back to Las Vegas, I know I'm going to be horribly 'homesick.' My family will wish I'd never gone away."

"Tell us about them," his uncle persisted in a kindly voice. Gaby could feel Luke's unsettling glance. He made it difficult for her to gather her thoughts.

"There are six children, five boys and myself."

Everyone expressed surprise over so many boys. "Are you the oldest?"

"No. I'm number four. Scott, my brother who is two years my senior, is the only one married so far."

"Are your parents living?"

"Yes. Mother teaches resource at a local junior high school."

"*Resource*?"

"Her mother helps students who have behavior problems, *Zio*," Giovanni explained.

"That must be difficult work."

"It is," Gaby agreed. "But very rewarding."

"And your father?"

"Daddy is a commercial artist who works in advertising."

"Are you an artist, too?" The older man appeared genuinely interested.

"Oh, no." She shook her head. "Daddy says I'm a dabbler. I have too many interests and will never master any of them."

"Don't be modest, *signorina*," a deep voice inserted. "There must be at least one subject you excel in."

"She excels at everything, *fratello*. I'm proud to announce that Gaby has received top grades in all her classes both here at the university and in Nevada. Like you, Luca, she thrives on learning."

Gaby flushed. "You love to exaggerate, and I am still struggling with Italian. It's such a beautiful language, but difficult. If I hadn't taken Latin in high school, I'd be lost. Thankfully, Giovanni has been helping me. If my Italian were half as good as the English you all speak, I'd be overjoyed."

"They teach Latin in Las Vegas?"

The question came from Giovanni's mother, changing the tenor of the conversation. It was the first time since they'd sat down to dinner that she'd spoken directly to Gaby.

Giovanni chuckled. "Of course they do, Mama."

"I can understand why you'd ask that question, Signora Provere. Most people consider Las Vegas a den of iniquity because of the legalized gambling. Many of us who live there avoid that part of town as much as possible. My parents don't gamble. They don't believe in it."

"It couldn't be a suitable place to raise children."

Giovanni patted his mother's hand. "That would all depend on the children, Mama. Gaby has grown up untouched by its influence."

His mother looked less than convinced.

"There are many evil influences in the world today, Signora Provere. Is any place truly safe except inside the walls of our own homes?" Gaby tried to reason with her.

Giovanni's uncle gave her a nod of approval. "You make a strong point, *signorina*."

Luke unexpectedly pushed himself away from the table and rose to his feet. "If you will all excuse me. There are matters I've left unattended too long as it is. *Buona notte*."

His parting salutation included everyone before he strode toward the doors with the bearing of a Medieval prince and disappeared.

Gaby had to pretend not to be affected, but his abrupt departure stunned her. He couldn't go yet! After a whole evening in his company, she still didn't know anything about him personally or professionally. He'd be returning to Rome in the morning. Day after tomorrow she'd be leaving Italy.

What if she never saw him again? In a short account of time he'd become so important to her, she couldn't imagine not being in his company again.

Something had to be wrong with her to care this much about a man she'd only known a few hours. In one meeting, the kinds of feelings he engendered were tantamount to being in love....

She'd always scoffed at the idea of love at first sight. But tonight, through some unfathomable process, she was very much afraid she'd lost her heart to one Luca Provere.

"Gaby?" *Giovanni's voice.* "I know tomorrow is a big day for you, so if you are through, I'll run you back to your *pensione.*"

He must have picked up on her distress. Had her feelings for Luke been so transparent he could sense her interest in his mysterious brother?

Mortified, she rose to her feet at the same time as Giovanni and turned to his mother. "Signora Provere, thank you for allowing me to be a guest in this magnificent palazzo. Of all my memories of Urbino, this evening will stand out as the highlight."

"*Prego*, Signorina Holt." She sounded less than enthusiastic, but it didn't seem to bother Giovanni.

Attempting to hide her desolation that Luke was no longer in the room, Gaby smiled at the other members of his family, even Efresina who'd said nothing for the last fifteen minutes and refused to look at Gaby. "It was a great pleasure meeting all of you."

For the most part they reciprocated in an affectionate fashion. Though gratified by their acceptance, Gaby could take little pleasure in anything when the man who'd brought her senses alive was nowhere to be found.

To her chagrin, she wasn't allowed to escape the room unscathed. The last thing she saw as she went out the doors were Luke's black eyes staring out of the massive portrait. They seemed to follow her through the maze of rooms to the front entrance of the castle.

"W-will your brother be driving us again?"

"Gaby—" He cocked his head. "You aren't still afraid of him, are you?"

"Of course not." She tried to keep the tremor out of her voice.

Giovanni eyed her speculatively. "Then you must be nervous about my driving. If you would feel safer with him behind the wheel, I will go to his apartments and ask him."

"*No*! Please don't!" she cried in panic. "I—I was only wondering, since he drove us here in the first place."

Seemingly satisfied with her explanation, Giovanni led her down the steps to the waiting black sedan. Once they were both seated inside he confided, "If Luca acts pensive and forbidding, it's because he has a great deal on his mind these days. After a year's absence, he's needed to come home and be surrounded by family."

Luke has been away a whole year?

"He's concerned for your welfare, Giovanni." She might as well broach the subject which had been put off too long as it was.

"I know. That has always been his way. He makes everyone else's world right, but rarely does anything to please himself."

"Obviously you two share a very special bond."

"I idolize him."

She bit her lip. "In all these weeks that we've known each other, you've never talked about him. Why?"

"Because it's painful."

By now they'd left the castle grounds and had entered the mainstream of heavy traffic.

Gaby didn't understand. "In what way?"

"You saw the painting in the dining room."

"Yes." She bowed her head. "Except for the clothes, it could have been your brother."

"Exactly. Almost from the day he was born, my parents thought the same thing. They saw our great progenitor in his face and body. Luke is a brilliant scholar with a keen mind and a grasp of the political and economic scene given to few men. It was a foregone conclusion that one day he would consecrate his life to God and rise to power like our illustrious forebearer."

Gaby blinked. *What was he saying?*

The Luke she'd met tonight was a sensual man, the ultimate male, the antithesis of someone celibate. He had a way of bringing out her most primitive feelings.

Yet snatches of conversation came back to haunt her. Luke lived in Rome. He had his work there. Giovanni kept referring to him as *fratello*, that he trusted him with his life.

Dear God. The shock of his words immobilized her. She dreaded asking the next question, but her curiosity had reached its zenith.

"Are you telling me he's a *priest*?"

Giovanni nodded slowly. "He's been training for the priesthood all his life, but father's death required that he put his church studies aside temporarily to run the estate.

"A year ago, when he felt I could handle things, he went to Rome to live and prepare himself. He'll be professed at the end of September on his twenty-ninth birthday."

It was too late for Gaby to stifle her gasp. This man she'd been fantasizing about was on the verge of becoming an ordained priest!

He'd be known as Father Luca. She'd never see him again. He'd be lost to her forever . . .

Gaby wanted to run somewhere and hide her feelings from Giovanni, but she couldn't. The car was stuck in traffic. More people than ever were out on the streets celebrating. This should have been her happiest night abroad, but Giovanni's news had robbed her of her joie de vivre.

"It's a miracle my brother was allowed to come to Urbino for twenty-four hours."

Not a miracle, she mused brokenheartedly. Luke left his life's work to check on the unsuitable American woman whom he believed would cast his brother aside when she'd gotten what she wanted out of him.

Now that Luke had met Gaby, he knew differently, and could return to Rome content that she wouldn't destroy Giovanni's life.

Had she made any impression at all on his older brother? Or was she reading something into those few precious moments when his smoldering looks melted her bones? Was it possible she would haunt his dreams as surely as he was going to haunt hers?

Gaby didn't think she could stand any more of this, especially when there was a vital issue that needed to be discussed with Giovanni.

Turning to him, she murmured, "Your brother loved you enough to make the effort to come home."

"Yes," came the solemn reply. "I should be grateful. One day Luca will wear scarlet robes. On rare occasions, I'll be lucky to be granted an audience to see him." There was deep pain in Giovanni's voice.

"You've missed him terribly, haven't you?"

He nodded.

Gaby could understand that. She already ached over Luke's absence. It was easy enough to picture him dressed in a cardinal's robes. He was a beautiful male specimen. Any clothes he wore would transform them.

But her heart couldn't imagine him living the life of a priest, let alone a cardinal or any other holy office. Since the first moment she'd laid eyes on him, she'd thought of him as a man who lived life to the fullest, who would crave the intimacy with his wife and rejoice in his children.

All this time she'd been afraid another woman had possession of his heart. Now to learn that long ago the church had laid claim to his body and soul—

"I feel the same way about my brother, Wayne. I adore him. But he works on a ranch in the Sierra Nevadas. I hardly ever see him."

"Is your brother happy working on a ranch?"

Gaby didn't have to think. "It's his life!"

"Then even if you miss him, it is easy for you to be happy for him."

"Yes, of course."

She pushed some stray tendrils off her forehead with a shaky hand. "What are you getting at? Are you saying that your brother isn't happy?" she asked with a heavy heart.

"I don't know. He isn't one to share anything that personal."

Her throat swelled with emotion. "He says you're a very private person, too." She looked at him, gearing up her courage. "Giovanni—I have to ask you a question. Please don't take it wrong. When you called him to come home, did you tell him you were going to marry me?" She had to know the truth.

"No."

The relief of hearing his admission was exquisite.

"But he and your mother are under that impression."

"That's because I love you. If I were to marry, I would ask you to be my wife, not Efresina, the woman my mother has picked out for me. Luca could sense this without my having to say anything. He's intuitive that way.''

Gaby's nails bit into her palms. Luke had been right all along about his brother's feelings for her!

"Do not worry, Gaby. I know you don't care about me that way, but it was still important to me that my family meet you.''

"I love you, too, Giovanni—as a dear friend.'' Her voice caught. How cruel that she couldn't have reciprocated by wanting to stay in Italy and marry him.

"I'm aware of that, and I'm hoping that when you get back to Las Vegas, you will remember the good times we had together. Perhaps by next summer, you will miss me enough to return to Urbino. Who knows what could happen by then.''

There can't be anything between us but friendship, she mused. His brother had created a fever in her. Priest or no priest, while Gaby was feeling this way about Luke, she could never marry anyone.

"Giovanni—''

"Do not feel obliged to say anything,'' he broke in. "It was enough to have you in my home tonight. You were gracious and kind to my mother. She, on the other hand, behaved poorly. She's lost one son and is holding on to me for dear life. Please forgive her.''

"I do. She wants the best for you.''

Gaby's heart swelled with compassion for his mother, for him. Without Luke, she imagined a lot of joy had gone out of their lives.

"Your maturity and generosity are some of the many traits I find so appealing about you. Luke must have approved or he wouldn't have excused himself for the night without talking privately to me first. It makes me very happy to know that my two favorite people got along. You did like him, didn't you?"

He honked at a group of students blocking the street. They finally realized he wanted to get through and moved to the side.

"Yes, of course," she said in a tremulous voice.

"Luca has always been protective. Because I'm short, he championed me when I got into trouble with my friends, then took the blame from our parents even though I should have been the one to be punished."

Everything he said made her heartache deepen. She smiled sadly. "Somehow I can't picture you a troublemaker."

"My father would tell you I had my moments, but a fatal stroke took him in my early teens. If it hadn't been for Luca, I would never have passed chemistry or understood philosophy. He had this wonderful mind, Gaby. He could do anything, be anything he wants."

There it was again. A big question mark in Giovanni's voice. As they turned into the alley at the back of the *pensione*, Gaby eyed her friend soberly.

"What is it you're saying, Giovanni? Don't you want him to serve the church?"

He pulled the car to a stop and turned off the motor. Still staring ahead he said, "More than anything on earth. But only if it's what he wants."

She was listening with her mind as well as her heart. That vital organ had given her no rest with its relentless pounding. "You don't think it's what he wants?"

"I don't know. Luca is a noble human being."

A long silence stretched between them. Gaby thought back on their conversation about his parents' lofty dreams for their firstborn son. No doubt Giovanni was thinking of them, too.

Taking a steadying breath, she said, "Your brother strikes me as a man who makes his own fires, who walks to the beat of his own drum, no one else's."

He turned his head in her direction and smiled. "You understand a great deal for having known him such a short time. And you're right about him. He's his own man and always will be. I don't know what got into me. I guess he and I are both in the habit of worrying too much about each other."

"My brothers and I do the same thing. You should have heard the lecture I got from Wayne before I left home."

Giovanni's eyes gleamed. "About Italian men?"

"About men, period. My brother, Scott, has already told the family that I'm just like our great-grandmother. That the Italian in my blood is going to make me fall for some foreign, godlike, down-and-out Lothario and I'll never come home again. Robbie phones me every week to make sure I'm still here."

"I'm glad they care so much, Gaby."

She nodded. "I am, too."

Giovanni was in a mood to talk. Normally she would have loved nothing better. But that was before Luke's advent into her life. Right now she needed to be by herself. The revelations about him had turned her world inside out. She felt like she'd just lived through an earthquake and was still experiencing aftershocks.

"Giovanni—thank you for a magical night. I'll never forget it."

"That's good. Now, before I let you go, I have something to give you. I want you to wear it when we go to the masked ball at the university tomorrow night."

He reached into the glove compartment and pulled out what looked like an antique porcelain jewelry box. When he opened it, her eyes widened in disbelief.

"That's the Renaissance hair piece! The one out of the collection at the museum!"

"The exact one."

"I couldn't, Giovanni. It's a family treasure."

His hands moved apart expressively. "What are treasures for if they can't be worn once in a while? Your hair is perfect for it. Please do this for me? I've never asked a favor of you before."

The night had brought many shocks which had left her drained and in pain. At such a low ebb, the hint of pleading in his tone was more than she could handle. Giovanni was determined to turn tomorrow night into another unforgettable highlight of her trip to Italy.

But she couldn't imagine finding any happiness knowing that Luke would be back in Rome. Though only two hours away by car, he might as well be on another planet as live at the Vatican. Not even his own family would have the right to visit him unless it was a matter of life and death.

Yet his leaving Urbino in the morning was creating a life and death situation for her. How would she ever get over him? She'd never met a man like him. She never would again. Tonight he'd left the table before she was prepared to let him go. If she could see him one more time, talk to him a little more...

"Giovanni," she murmured, "I'd be honored to wear this hair jewelry, but I don't have the faintest idea how to put it on. I'd need help, and don't trust anyone here."

"*Bene.* One of the maids, Luciana, often does my mother's hair when her own stylist isn't available. She will be delighted to assist you."

"It would have to be early in the morning because the rest of my day will be taken up with packing and getting ready to go home. The thing is, I realize y-your brother," she stammered, "is going back to Rome tomorrow and I would hate to intrude on your private family time."

Even as she said it, Gaby prayed to be forgiven for mentioning Luke, for still wanting him. He was on the brink of taking solemn vows which prohibited him from having a relationship with a woman. She was going to have to forget him, put him out of her mind. *But how*? her heart repeated the question over and over again.

"You couldn't intrude if you wanted to. I'll come for you at six-thirty. We'll go back to the palace and have breakfast together. Luca wants to be away by eight. Then Luciana can see to your hair."

Breakfast with Luke? A sudden rush of adrenaline made her want to jump out of her skin.

"I'll be ready," she said in a breathless voice. "Please keep the jewelry with you. It's far too valuable. I'd die if anything happened to it." She left the box on the seat.

He eyed her with a pensive expression. "No earthly treasure is worth dying for, Gaby. Now a sacred love, that's something else again."

She averted her eyes. Something told her Giovanni knew about her secret attraction to Luke. With those cryptic words, he intended to crush any thoughts she might be entertaining about his brother whose heart embraced a higher form of love.

She wondered if this had happened before—Giovanni bringing home a girl, only to have her fall in love with Luke. It was a horrifying thought. She felt so ashamed and so helpless.

"Good night, Giovanni."

"*Buona notte*, Gaby."

She slid from the car, shut the door and waved until he'd left the alley.

The happy girl who'd left earlier in the evening to enjoy the Renaissance Fair was not the same troubled woman who entered the back door of the *pensione*, wondering how life would ever hold the same meaning for her again.

She could return home to live in Nevada, surrounded by her loved ones. She could even find a way to move to this region of Italy, a part of her heritage. There was no more beautiful spot on earth. But either way she would be empty because of a man she'd only known three hours.

Whatever it was about Luke, meeting him had altered her life drastically. He was a man whose mere presence defined the role of woman in her as no one else had ever done or would do. A man to whom she felt bonded though his destiny lay in an entirely different direction.

Perhaps Scott was right and she had more of her great-grandmother in her than she had supposed. Gabriella Trussardi had lost her heart to a vagabond artist and had followed him literally to the ends of the earth.

Gaby Holt would do the same thing for the love of one Luca Provere. But where he went, she couldn't follow. Even if he weren't a priest, she had no right to love him. Not when his brother had met and loved her first.

Intense pain propelled her up the stairs to her room. Most of the students were still enjoying the fair. With sleep out of the question, she could get her house cleaning done for the next occupant without disturbing anyone.

After changing into a baggy T-shirt and cutoffs, she plunged in. The key was to keep busy until she dropped from exhaustion.

A half hour later, Gaby needed to escape the heat and went to the study-hall-cum-salon for an Orangina. There was no such a thing as ice, but at least it would be wet and quench her thirst.

To her surprise she found a roomful of students who lived at the *pensione*. They were huddled together in serious conversation, gesticulating back and forth. She heard smatterings of German and French.

Celeste motioned to Gaby the second she saw her. "You have heard the news, *oui*?"

She came to a standstill. "No."

"Aie... An accident down the street. You know? *Une auto, écrasée. Mon Dieu, c'est affreux*."

Perhaps she was being paranoid, but Gaby found herself asking, "What color was the car?"

"*Noire*," Lise supplied. "Black. It came from *le palais*."

Not Giovanni... "That's my friend's car. Where did it happen?" Gaby cried in alarm.

After a discussion, the girls decided it would be easier to show her. Frantic, Gaby dashed from the room following the others to the front door of the *pensione*.

But once she gained the outside, her progress was blocked by a cobalt blue Maserati which had just pulled up to the entry. The bricked street was too narrow for cars to park, which meant she and her friends had to walk around it.

Gaby tried to dodge the person getting out of the driver's side and found herself face to face with the man who had transformed her life.

"*Luke*!"

Only the most tragic news would have brought him here. She felt the blood drain from her face. On cue, her legs started to give way.

With a fierce explanation he gripped her shoulders to prevent her from falling. "Gabriella," he said her name for the first time in the Italian way, giving her a little shake.

She tried to talk coherently. "The girls—they just told me about Giovanni— They were taking me to the scene of the accident."

His eyes penetrated the darkened blue of hers. "There would be no point. I've just come from the hospital. He's had a concussion, but he's going to be all right."

His words brought blessed relief. Gaby sagged against him. "Thank heaven his injuries weren't more serious," she cried softly, not realizing what she was saying or doing until her lips grazed the gold cross hanging around his neck.

The metal, warm from his hard body, scorched her. She sprang apart from him, guilt ridden and humiliated by her lack of control.

"I—I'm sorry. Please forgive me," she begged, her emotions in utter chaos. "I didn't mean—"

"There's nothing to forgive." His voice grated. "My brother has given us too many surprises for one night. Is there anything you need before I drive you to the hospital? Giovanni wants to see you."

Trying to think, she backed away from him, still unsteady. His gaze lowered to take in her attire. The blood returned to her cheeks with alarming swiftness.

She would never have worn this outfit in front of a man, let alone Luca Provere. Loose as it was, the thin cotton T-shirt revealed far too much of her figure. The cutoffs accentuated her long, elegant legs.

"I need to change," her voice trailed before she disappeared inside the *pensione*, only to face a barrage of questions from her friends. They followed her to her room.

While she put on the clothes she'd worn to dinner, they commiserated over Giovanni's accident. But what they really wanted to talk about was the gorgeous male specimen sitting outside in the Maserati.

The questions flew, but Gaby was too overwhelmed by Luke's appearance at the *pensione* to satisfy their curiosity. All she knew was that he made an unforgettable impact on anyone who met him.

She would never have wished for more time alone with him at the expense of Giovanni's physical wellbeing, but her heart didn't seem to know that. She couldn't remember her feet touching the ground as she made her way out the door to his car.

CHAPTER FOUR

GABY could hear the motor idling as she slid inside the luxury sports car. Luke had left the passenger door open and reached across her body to shut it once she was seated.

As he fastened the lap belt, his arm accidentally brushed against her midriff. The disturbing contact sent a prickle of expectancy through her system. Before directing his attention to the road, he slanted her a probing glance that left her dazed.

She linked her fingers together. "H-how did the accident happen?" Giovanni hadn't seemed upset when he'd left her, but now she knew differently. She'd been riddled with guilt since the moment the girls had told her about it.

"He had to swerve to avoid a group of students and crashed into a wall. I expect there'll be bruises, but on the whole, he was lucky to escape without getting himself killed."

"Your poor mother must be frantic."

He geared down to take a curve, controlling the powerful engine with practiced ease. "That's one way of putting it. Giovanni never was a good driver."

"Did—did you see the car?"

His jaw hardened. "If you mean what was left of it, yes. We can thank God it happened after he brought you back to the *pensione*."

The words he left out created a horrifying picture in her mind. Gaby shivered convulsively. "I-it's my fault he's hurt," she said in a tortured whisper.

With a grimace, Luke maneuvered the car to the casualty parking area of the hospital and shut off the motor. "So you did confront him."

She bent her head. "Yes."

"Did he admit to wanting to marry you?" Luke demanded in clipped tones.

Gaby wiped her eyes with the palms of her hands. "H-he said that if he did marry, I was the woman he would choose, but he knew I didn't feel the same way about him. He's h-hoping I'll miss him and come back next summer."

The man next to her stirred restlessly. "And what was your response?"

"I told him I cared for him very much, but beyond that, I—I didn't know what to say."

She heard a harsh intake of breath. "He's still in the denial phase of your rejection."

Her head jerked toward him. "What do you mean?"

"He asked me to bring you to him. You're the only person he wants to see."

"I don't understand."

Luke flexed his hand. "He refuses to talk to Mother or me."

She was staggered by the revelation. "This is a nightmare. Luke, you have to believe I never meant to hurt him. He's a good friend. That's all!"

"You and I both know that," he rasped, "but love can change a man beyond recognition." The timbre of his voice revealed new layers of pain.

"If I'd had any idea—" she cried, shaking her head in disbelief.

She heard his muttered imprecation. "I thought I knew my brother, but I returned home to find a stranger inhabiting his body."

"I—I don't know what to do. The last thing I want is to make the situation worse. If I refuse to see h—"

"You won't refuse," he asserted the avowal. "His doctor says he mustn't be upset right now. Once more I'm going to have to ask you to play a part."

She let out a groan. "For how long?"

His dark eyes impaled her. "For as long as it takes," came the grating voice. He levered himself from the driver's seat.

She knew his hand at her elbow was an impersonal gesture to assist her from the car. Yet despite the precarious circumstances of Giovanni's accident, her body felt electrified by his touch. Somehow he must have sensed her reaction because he reeled away from her the second she was on her feet.

Following a few steps behind him, she entered the emergency room. The place swarmed with friends and relatives of victims brought in for treatment. She supposed the fair had produced an influx of casualties. When she thought of Giovanni's brush with death, another shudder attacked her.

"This way," he murmured. Together they proceeded past various cubicles to the end where a blue curtain had been drawn. With every step, the sounds and smells started to get to her and she felt sick.

"Wait—" She grabbed his forearm for support.

"*Mio Dio!*" he importuned before putting his arm around her shoulders. "You've gone white as alabaster."

"Just give me a moment," she whispered. For a time she was out of control of her actions. Until her ears stopped buzzing, she clung to him. Slowly the warmth and reassurance of his hard body seeped into hers. She became aware of other sensations which had no place at a time like this, let alone with a man like Luca Provere.

Beneath his black silk shirt, her cheek registered the strong pounding of his heart. Like a person under water, all her movements were slow as she reluctantly began drawing away from him. When her hands slid from his chest, she felt the tremor of his powerful body with a sense of wonder.

He stared at her balefully. "You're not up to this. I'm going to take you back to the *pensione.*"

Out of self-preservation, she put some distance between them. "No— I—I'm all right. Giovanni is the one we have to think about right now." Without waiting to hear what his response would be, she moved to the edge of the curtain and pulled it aside.

"*Gaby!*"

"Oh, Giovanni. What have you done to yourself?" His forehead was wrapped to hold some gauzy pads over the spot where he must have hit the windshield. He couldn't have been wearing a seat belt. But other than the injury to his head, he looked in surprisingly good shape.

She rested her cheek tenderly against his for a brief moment, then raised back up. "You look younger dressed in that hospital gown. I can picture you the way you must have been as a boy."

He laughed. Thank heavens he still could. "I feel like a little boy with the staff waiting on me."

Tears stung her eyes. "I'm so grateful you're all right. When Lu—" She stopped, then started again. "When your brother came to find me and told me what happened, I was shocked. Are you in a lot of pain?"

"Not very much. Mostly I am ashamed to have wrecked the car. This is not my first accident."

"Compared to your life, a car means nothing. Giovanni—" She lowered her voice. "What's wrong? Your brother tells me you've refused to talk to him or your mother. Don't you know how much that hurts them?"

"Are they both here?"

"I haven't seen your mother, but Luke is right outside."

A sleepy smile broke out on his face. "Do you really call him Luke?"

She colored. "I—I didn't mean to, especially when I know he's about to become Father Luca. It just sort of slipped out. I'm afraid I'm very typical of my nationality. We don't often stand on formality."

"It's a refreshing change, Gaby. I'm sure he thinks so, too. Tell him to come in."

She blinked. "Now?"

"Yes."

Relieved for Luke, she murmured, "I'll get him."

Patting his arm, she slipped outside the curtain. Luke stood a little ways off, his head bent in deep concentration. It gave her immense satisfaction just to look at him. What would it be like to feast her eyes on him forever, and have the right to do it?

"Luke?" she called his name softly. At the sound of her voice he turned. His eyes were dark and brooding on her face. "He wants to see you."

A stillness came over him as he continued to study her without giving away anything of what he was thinking. She grew uneasy before he indicated that he was coming. When she returned to Giovanni's bedside, Luke wasn't far behind. He walked around to the other side of the bed so he was facing her.

Giovanni stared at his brother with a look of such love, Gaby's heart swelled with emotion. "*Fratello*— You know Mama. She asks so many questions. Tonight I'm too tired to answer them. That is why I didn't want her here. At times like this, you are the only one who can help calm her down.

"As for Gaby, I thought if you brought her to the hospital, then I would only have to say things *once* to the both of you."

Luke's face was grim with concern. "Has the doctor found further injuries? Tell me!" His voice rang with love. Theirs was a rare, special bond between brothers.

"No. But he says I must stay in the hospital for observation at least two days. Gaby—" His heavy-lidded brown eyes slowly shifted to her. "I am sorry I won't be able to take you to the ball. I know how much you were counting on it."

Her hands spread apart emotively. "How can you even think about it at a time like this? I couldn't care less, Giovanni. All that matters is that you get well."

"What ball are you talking about?" Luke muttered in a low voice.

Gaby shook her head. "It's nothing. Forget it."

"The Renaissance ball held at the university," Giovanni persisted. "It's the culminating activity of Gaby's art history studies. Everything will be authentic. This is a once-in-a-lifetime opportunity for her. I wanted her to wear an authentic hair piece in honor of the event." Giovanni spoke to his brother as if she weren't in the room.

"It's over there in a bag the ambulance people brought in. The porcelain box was smashed at impact, but the jewelry wasn't damaged."

Like someone in slow motion, Luke found the bag sitting on a chair and lifted out the contents. When he examined the elaborate pearl headdress, she didn't think his eyes could go any darker, but they did.

Clearly shocked, his gaze flickered immediately to his brother, sending him an unspoken message she couldn't decipher. Giovanni didn't appear in the least affected by Luke's reaction.

"I planned to bring Gaby to the palace in the morning so Luciana could arrange it in her hair. It goes perfectly with the dress I'd picked out for her."

"*What dress*?" Gaby was nonplussed.

His eyes closed. Fatigue had taken hold of him. "It was going to be another surprise."

She hugged her arms to her body. "I think there have been enough of those for one day."

"If only you weren't going back to Rome in the morning, Luca, you could take Gaby in my place. Then I wouldn't have to disappoint her when she has been looking forward to tomorrow night since her arrival in Urbino."

"That's not true!" she cried, aghast at such a suggestion. "Do you honestly think I could enjoy myself knowing you are lying hurt in a hospital?"

"I am not on my death bed, Gaby. In two, three days, I will be up and around again. But you will never come back to Urbino. Deep down in my heart I know that now. That's why I want your last night here to be one you'll remember forever."

In the most gracious way possible, Giovanni had just told her in front of his brother that he'd accepted her rejection of him.

Luke's eyes captured hers, the throbbing nerve in his jaw clearly visible. "Tomorrow night is your last night?" he inquired in his deep voice.

"Yes. School is over. My tour bus leaves for Belgium day after tomorrow. I'll be flying from Brussels to the States." I'll never see you again, Luca Provere. *Why does that fact hurt me so much?* she groaned inwardly.

Breaking eye contact with him, she leaned over Giovanni and gave him a kiss on the cheek. "I'll call tomorrow to see how you are getting along. Since your brother is leaving in the morning, I'm going to go now so the two of you can enjoy the precious little time you have left together."

"I'll drive you, then come back," Luke announced as if it were a foregone conclusion.

"No." She shook her head emphatically. "I'm so relieved Giovanni is all right, I feel like walking."

Luke's features looked chiseled. He wasn't used to being dictated to. "It's getting late. You shouldn't be out on the streets alone.'' He didn't let up in order to emphasize the point.

She smiled bravely at him. The way she was feeling about him right now, there was much less danger mixing with the crowd. ''Tonight everyone is out! My *pensione* is only ten minutes from here. I need to walk off that fabulous dinner and I'd like to stretch my legs.''

Giovanni sighed. There were purple smudges beneath his closed lids. ''Do not argue with Gaby, my dear Luca. She is an independent American woman who knows her own mind and can protect herself. When a scoundrel tried to pick her pocket two weeks ago, she did a trick that made him double over, then run off. Something her brothers taught her.''

Luke didn't appear impressed or convinced.

''*Buona notte*, Giovanni.''

''*Buona notte*, Gaby.''

She moved to the curtain, then paused. ''It was a pleasure meeting you, Signore Provere.'' She fought to keep her voice steady. ''Have a nice trip back to Rome. *Arriverderla*.''

She hurried out of the cubicle and down the crowded hall to the doors, having no idea if he'd said goodbye or not. But she didn't dare stay to find out.

Once she reached the outside, she broke into a run. Thank heaven it was dark and the streets were starting to empty. She didn't want her glistening cheeks to attract any more attention than necessary.

All the way back to the *pensione* she turned over the night's earthshaking events in her mind. If she knew Giovanni, he'd send a car for her in the morning and follow through on all his good intentions. He'd probably dredge up one of his friends to take her to the ball.

This time she was one step ahead of him. Of course she wouldn't leave Urbino without saying goodbye. But she'd do that tomorrow night.

Tonight she would get all her packing done, then be up at daybreak. If she took the first bus leaving Urbino, she could spend the morning in Assisi and the afternoon in Loretello. By nightfall her bus would bring her back to town in time to check in on Giovanni. It would be hard to say goodbye for the last time. Under the circumstances, she felt it wise to keep her visit short.

The problem was, there was no way she could stay in Urbino tomorrow knowing that Luke had gone to Rome. She needed to exorcize him from her heart. The best way to do that was to keep busy and fill her mind with new sights and experiences.

The trip to Belgium through Switzerland and France would help. When she got back to Las Vegas, she'd take a quarter off of school and ask Wayne if she could come and work for him on the ranch. No more Italian for her. She'd fulfilled her promise to her great-grandmother. That part of her education was finished.

When Gaby finally got back to the *pensione*, she met Celeste in the hall on the way to her room.

"Eh, Gaby. How is your friend?"

"He's going to be all right."

"*Grace à Dieu*." She cocked her brunette head. "And the other one who is so *magnifique*?"

"He leaves for Rome in the morning."

Her brows frowned dramatically. "So you won't see him again?"

"No."

"*Quelle catastrophe!*"

"It doesn't matter, Celeste. I'll be leaving for home on Sunday."

"Do you want to come with us tomorrow? I don't know what we're planning, but we will amuse ourselves, *n'est-ce pas?*"

"Thanks. I appreciate the invitation, but I'm going to go away for the day."

"*Pourquoi?* The fair is still on! Where will you go?"

"I—I'm not sure yet," Gaby prevaricated. Celeste was a nice girl, but if Giovanni had a car sent for Gaby from the palace and the driver discovered she wasn't at the *pensione*, he'd inquire as to her whereabouts. The always helpful Celeste would be the first person to give information. Tomorrow was one time when Gaby didn't want to be found.

"Good night. Thanks for caring."

"*Bien sur.* We are friends, *non?* I must find out where you live before you leave. My parents are planning a trip to Los Angeles, Disneyland, next year. You are close, *oui?*"

"Kind of." Gaby smiled sadly. "I'll be back tomorrow night. We'll exchange addresses then."

"*Tres bien. Bonne nuit, chérie.*"

The Medieval town of Assisi rested on an Umbrian hilltop shrouded in early morning mist. Gaby's first view of the ancient citadel was so lovely, so *Italian*, it made her want to cry all over again.

She'd shed many tears on the two-hour drive from Urbino. With every zigzagging kilometer, the rolling landscape of green hills and valleys thrilled her heart. Each knoll revealed oak and poplar-lined river banks, walled towns, lush orchards. No matter where she looked she saw well-ordered farms, crenelated castles, chains of undulating pastoral countryside dotted with vineyards.

Until she'd met Luke, Gaby couldn't understand how her great-grandmother had left the charm and color of a region so exquisite it looked like a Renaissance painting come to life, for the love of a man.

To Gaby it was frightening to realize that such a powerful love could sweep you away so that nothing else mattered but to be with that one human being who colored your world for all time.

Luke had colored hers. She'd never be the same again and wondered if he thought of her at all. Last night there'd been certain charged moments when she'd felt a chemistry so strong, she'd grown sick with excitement. If he'd felt it, too, then how did he deal with his forbidden thoughts? How did he put them away? She'd like to know his secret.

By now he was back in Rome, swallowed up in a life she couldn't comprehend.

"*Signorina*?"

Startled, Gaby glanced at the driver. He was signaling that she should get off. Their bus had entered the parking lot below the town.

Embarrassed to have delayed him, she hurried down the aisle and stepped to the ground, congratulating herself on getting away from Urbino before anyone had seen her to ask questions she had no desire to answer.

A local hotel several blocks' distance from the *pensione* catered to tourists and started serving breakfast at six. Gaby had walked there and sipped cappuccino while she waited for the bus which had taken her to a town further south. From there she'd caught another bus for Assisi.

Other tourists had the same idea. The parking lot had started to fill with the kind of tour buses she'd be taking to Belgium. This was her last day in Italy. Though her emotions were in chaos and her pain almost unendurable, she would give herself the gift of this day.

Inhaling the soft air sweetened by the fragrance from surrounding fruit farms, she set off to visit the holy abode of the legendary St. Francis of Assisi.

On the way up the many steps, she moved past groups of nuns and priests who'd come on pilgrimage to the sacred shrine. She tried to imagine Luke among them and couldn't, probably because she was in denial over his life's work.

Angry with herself for continuing to dwell on him, she went first to the dark, claustrophobic area under the church where St. Francis was purported to be buried. Then she ascended to the basilica to view the priceless frescoes.

Gregorian chant filled the nave. In the past, she enjoyed hearing priests sing their ancient music. But today the haunting sounds drove her from the church.

The mist had started to burn off, revealing a blue sky. Hoping it was a good omen, Gaby pushed forward, exploring the mazelike town with its cobblestoned pathways and hidden churches tucked away in mellowed-orange walls.

A ten minute walk from the main piazza, she came across many separate flights of stairs which she ascended. At the top, she spied the watch towers of a castle in the distance and was drawn to it.

Eventually she reached her destination and paid the fee to enter the Rocca Maggiore. Free to wander around the outer bailey, she tried to imagine herself as a knight.

Unfortunately the only picture that came to mind was a vision of Luke, his dark head thrown back, his black eyes flashing as his man-at-arms helped to dress his incredible male body in battle armor.

Praying to rid his image from her heart, she moved through a dark corridor punctuated every so often by arrow slits. The staircase at the other end was pitch black. She'd have to feel her way if she wanted to go any further.

Determined to make it all the way, she started the climb. Round and round she went, half fearing she might bump into someone coming down. But she couldn't hear any sounds except her own footsteps. Finally she gained the top.

What she saw when she walked to the edge of the tower defied description. Ripple after ripple of meadow and farm delineated by hedges and tree rows stretched to the horizon. Every direction delighted the eye. She stood there for ages. This was a degree of beauty unmatched anywhere in the world.

"An anonymous poet once wrote that this region of Italy is the view from God's window. The soul of anyone trespassing here will go away enlarged."

Gaby had been standing with her hands on the ledge, her face raised to the sun. She'd been enjoying the slight breeze which wafted through her waist-long hair, lifting it from the sides of her damp neck. At the sound of the distinctive male voice coming from behind, she let out a small cry and her fingers dug into the stone parapet till one of them drew blood.

She had to be hallucinating and was afraid to turn around. Wanting Luke had become an obsession. Now her mind had conjured him up!

Knowing he was in Rome, Gaby worried that she might be on the brink of a nervous breakdown. In an effort to get control of herself, she remained in place, not trusting her senses.

"Giovanni told me you were a little frightened of me. I didn't take him seriously, but now I'm beginning to wonder." His wry tone caught her off guard.

Dear God. It *was* Luke. Shock made her breath come in pants. "W-what are you d-doing here?"

"You may well ask," he murmured cryptically. "You're as unpredictable as you are impulsive."

She whirled around. While her eyes were adjusting to the shaded area where he stood tall and dark in a charcoal shirt and trousers, she could feel his intent gaze roving over her face and body. She sensed he was making comparisons between her attire of last night and today.

In keeping with the hot summer weather, she'd worn a sensible pale blue cotton wraparound skirt and a white, short-sleeved top. Her Italian leather sandals had been everywhere and looked good with anything she wore. But when Luke looked at her, she felt exposed and warm, as if he had the ability to see what lay beneath the surface and ferret her womanly secrets.

Her breathing grew shallow. "W-why aren't you in Rome?"

"Giovanni had a bad night."

"How bad?" she asked in a tremulous voice.

"He's suffering dizziness, which in turn has upset his stomach. The doctor says this is to be expected with a head injury. It will pass. But our mother is taking it rather badly."

"I don't blame her. Dear Giovanni."

"Under the circumstances, I couldn't leave. Particularly not when Giovanni made me promise to call at the *pensione* and drive you to the palace to get your hair done for the ball."

She knew it. She just hadn't realized that it would be *Luke* who was the driver. Her body quivered. "That's very sweet of him, but I'm the last person he should be worrying about. I'm sorry you've been put to so much trouble to track me down."

His lips twitched. "It was no trouble. All I had to do was make a few phone calls in the right places and I knew exactly where to find the woman my informants refer to as the *squisita testarossa* from America."

Gaby blushed to the roots of her hair to hear herself described that way. What a fool she'd been to think she could elude the long reach of the Provere influence. Luke commanded the instant respect and cooperation of everyone in the Marches.

She cleared her throat. "Last night you heard me tell Giovanni that I had no intention of going out tonight. He carries his sense of duty way too far," she grumbled.

"That's his nature," he said in thick tones. "I'm afraid in this case, however, you don't have a choice. I made a promise to be your escort."

"*No!*" Her fearful cry rang in the air and she staggered back until she felt the rough ledge through the thin material of her blouse.

She couldn't possibly dance with him. To know his touch one more time, to feel his hands on her body when she knew he was a priest, was asking too much. It would be disastrous. *It would be wrong.*

His brows drew together in a forbidding black line. "After rejecting his love, do you care so little about him that you would deny him this last request before you leave the country? I wouldn't have thought you of all people would purposely hinder his recovery."

Luke's hands had gone to his hips, forcing her to be even more aware of his devastating masculine appeal. Angry because of her futile attraction to him—stung by his cruel insinuations—she cried, "How can you say that to me? I'd do anything to help him get better. But to go to—"

"*Bene*." He prevented her from further remonstration. "Luciana will have an afternoon's work ahead of her confining all that hair in time for you to dress."

"No!" she cried again out of a sense of self-preservation.

He thrust her a long, unreadable glance.

She fiddled with the tie of her skirt nervously, unwittingly drawing his interest when she hadn't meant to. "I know what you promised Giovanni, a-and I certainly don't want to make his condition worse. But—" She paused to swallow. "I have no desire to attend a ball. That was always your brother's idea."

"He thought it would please you," came the wooden retort.

Guilt assailed her. "That's the problem. He tries too hard." Her voice quivered.

She felt his body tauten and knew she'd said the wrong thing, but now that she'd started this, she had to go on.

"T-there's something else I'd planned to do with my last few hours in Italy."

His sharp intake of breath warned her to tread carefully. "What would that be?"

"It's not your concern," she assured him in a meek tone, growing more uneasy by the minute. "The point is, he would never have to know about it. Not if we lied to him," she said in a small voice. "Just a little lie that would make us all happy."

"You're forgetting Luciana who will run to Giovanni if you don't show up. She adores him."

Gaby lifted pleading eyes to him. "You could explain to her that one of my friends at the *pensione* has insisted on helping me instead."

"He'll expect a full report after the ball."

"I realize that. Naturally I intended to say goodbye to him one last time. But you could put off your visit until tomorrow morning, couldn't you?"

"Our stories may not match," he persisted with maddening logic.

"Please—" she begged him.

The desperation in her voice must have reached him. He folded his arms, his eyes holding a strange glitter. "I might be willing to cooperate, provided you tell me what it is that's so important."

"After leaving here, I'd planned to go to Loretello one last time to see if I could find the farm that once belonged to my Trussardi relatives. I've had to budget my money, so I've only been out there once. But I never did find out any information. I speak a little Italian now, and hoped to talk to one of the old residents to see if they might remember something."

He ran a ringless hand through his black hair, signifying any number of emotions. "Why didn't you let Giovanni take you? He could have translated and been of enormous help."

She moistened her lips. "Because until last evening, I thought he was a poor, struggling student who didn't have enough money to buy me a *gelato*, let alone his own bus ticket," she added quietly when she saw the shadow that darkened Luke's face. "H-he was very resourceful and always found ways for us to enjoy ourselves without spending any lira at all."

"*Per Dio*!"

She winced from his anger. "I knew that if I told him about my frustration in not finding any information, he'd ask for time off from his work at the castle. That would mean he wouldn't earn as much take-home pay. Because he never talked about his family, I assumed they had few resources and that he was helping them out. Under the circumstances, I didn't want to place an unnecessary burden on him."

Luke's smothered epithet left her trembling. "I had no idea my brother could be this devious. He owes you an apology. So does my mother for treating you so abominably at dinner."

"No. It's not important." She shook her head, overwhelmed to elicit this kind of response from Luke. "We both know Giovanni meant no harm."

"Do we?" he asked in a voice she didn't recognize. "I'm afraid my feelings aren't that generous."

A troubling silence heightened her anxiety. "Don't be upset with your brother," she appealed to him. "He worships you. I honestly believe he'd throw himself off one of the palace towers if you suggested it. You know what a great tease Giovanni is. His pretense with me was nothing more than that. As you said yesterday, he has no guile.'

"I was wrong," Luke muttered with chilling ferocity. She hated being the cause of a rift between them and started to tell him so, but his next words stopped her.

"We'll drive to Loretello. By nightfall we ought to have located your relative's property. Come. I know a shortcut to the car."

CHAPTER FIVE

DAZED by the knowledge that Luke hadn't gone to
Rome, that instead, he had followed her to Assisi,
Gaby couldn't think clearly. Too late, she remem-
bered about the bus.

"Shouldn't I let the driver know I'm not riding
with him?"

She turned her head in the direction of the
parking area, inadvertently brushing the side of
Luke's face and neck with the ends of her hair.
Embarrassed because it hindered his vision, she
pulled the strands away as fast as she could.

"I already took care of it," came the husky rejoinder. As the Maserati began eating the kilo-
meters, she noted that his hands gripped the wheel
tighter. Already there was tension in the car and
they hadn't been in it five minutes.

Because of Giovanni, Luke's life had been thrown
off balance and he had every right to be upset. But
then, so had she.

This morning when she left Urbino, who would
have dreamed that by lunchtime she'd be ensconced in a fabulous Italian-made car, whizzing
through adorable towns in the Italian countryside
with Luca Provere?

She'd fallen in love with a man whose life was
dedicated to the church and it was killing her.

Gaby had never known anyone who had become a priest. Now would be her opportunity to ask questions and find out what spiritual forces had driven him to choose a vocation that denied him a life with a wife and family.

Had he never been in love? Didn't he wonder what it would be like to bring a son or daughter into the world?

Much as she wanted answers, she feared he would consider it an invasion of privacy. In fact, Giovanni had been so secretive with both her and Luke, it was possible Luke had no idea she knew he was about to take final vows.

Not that it would make any difference either way. But since Luke hadn't chosen to discuss anything of a personal nature with her, except where Giovanni was concerned, her instincts told her to say nothing.

"If you can wait another forty-five minutes, we'll come to a restaurant that serves a superb pasta dish called *vincisgrassi*, followed by fennel-stuffed rabbit that is out of this world."

"It sounds wonderful." Every minute she could spend alone with him was something to cherish.

"After we eat, we'll drive to Arcevia. That will be the spot where Loretello's civil and family group registries are located. We'll search the records and see if we can't come up with some information that will help you locate the plot of ground your great-grandparents once farmed."

"Why aren't the records kept in Loretello?"

"Like many Italian towns, it is too small to be what you Americans call the county seat."

"I had no idea." Her eyes fastened helplessly on his striking profile. "It sounds complicated and out of the way. I—I don't want to infringe on your time any more than I already have."

He darted her a shuttered glance. "I promised my brother to make your last day in Italy memorable. In my opinion, finding one's family roots takes precedence over attending a Renaissance ball, therefore I'm at your disposal."

"Thank you, Luke." Her voice caught. She looked away, afraid he'd see too much in her eyes. *This was her last day.* She couldn't bear to think of tomorrow without him.

"You don't need to thank me. To be honest, genealogical research has always intrigued me. You never know what kind of information will turn up."

"Well, it's certain there won't be a pope in *my* bloodline," she joked to cover her hectic emotions. "Probably just the opposite!"

His full-bodied laughter was the most thrilling sound she'd ever heard. She had the impression he hadn't let go and relaxed for a long, long time.

"With all that red hair, you could be right," he mocked dryly.

Heat swept through her body. "Maybe my great-grandmother didn't tell us the truth. Maybe she was trying to escape a bad home situation and ran off with the first person who could offer her freedom."

"Did she strike you as a woman with secrets?"

Gaby shook her head. "No. She seemed like a totally happy, fulfilled person, but then I was a child when she died."

"A child's instincts are rarely wrong."

"I don't know. Las Vegas is the antithesis of Loretello. I can't imagine her leaving this paradise unless she had to. You'd know what I meant if you'd ever traveled to Nevada."

"I've been there," he inserted quietly.

"*You*?"

Her astonishment produced another chuckle from him. "In my early twenties I traveled extensively in the United States which included an overnight stay in Las Vegas." Gaby would have been fourteen or fifteen, old enough to have developed a huge crush on him.

"I went on to school in California which gave me added time to explore. For someone from my country, the American desert has a beauty all its own."

She agreed with him, but the revelation that he'd once been that close to her made her blurt, "So *that's* why you speak English with hardly a trace of accent!"

"I'll take that as a compliment."

Gaby could scarcely credit they were talking to each other this way. She wanted the drive to last forever. "Did Giovanni accompany you? I don't recall him saying anything about it."

"No. He was too young. In any event, except for two months in England a few years ago when we went together at my instigation, he has never shown any inclination to stray far from home." Luke offered the information as if his brother's behavior continued to trouble him.

"I haven't known Giovanni long, but he seems very untouched by the world."

A strange sound came out of the man sitting next to her. "I thought so, too. That is, until he met you." His voice trailed off.

She didn't detect censure exactly. But there were undertones which filled her with trepidation. "I— I'll be gone tomorrow, out of his life."

"But not necessarily out of mind," he said rather intensely. "Unlike his friends, he never dated girls in his teens. In fact, he's never had a romantic interest in women and treats Efresina like a sister. That's why his phone call about you came as a complete shock—in more ways than one," he added cryptically.

Oddly enough, the news that Giovanni had never been attracted to women didn't surprise her. "From the beginning, your brother seemed to function on a different plane. That's the reason I enjoyed his company so much."

"So you used Giovanni for protection."

In an instant, the fragile rapport with him was gone. A tiny gasp escaped her throat. She jerked her head in his direction. "What do you mean?"

"Exactly what you think I meant," he said in a deceptively silken tone. "Let's not pretend you don't know the impact you make on the male population."

Incensed, she cried, "You say that as if it's a sin to be a woman!"

"It should be, when she looks like you," he grated. "Not even my brother was immune. The minute I saw you, I understood why."

Stunned into silence by his frank remarks, she watched dazedly as he pulled off the main road and entered the parking area of a quaint inn.

At one time the Trattoria Alberto must have been a small villa. Intimate tables for two with checkered cloths and pots of flowers placed in every conceivable nook beckoned diners to its trellised patio.

But Gaby no longer found joy in the surroundings, let alone their outing. In fact she felt ill. Her companion must have noticed because he didn't immediately get out of the car.

"You are the only woman of my acquaintance who could twist an innocent observation and make it sound like an insult."

"*Innocent*?" Her eyes glazed an incandescent blue. "You accused me of using Giovanni."

"Then you misunderstood me." His black eyes impaled her. "Let me rephrase it. Knowing that Giovanni would always remain the gentleman, you instinctively clung to him out of a sense of self-preservation. What an amazing irony that he turned out to be as vulnerable as the next man."

His explanation should have soothed her, but somehow it didn't. Gaby had trouble catching her breath and averted her eyes.

"American women unwisely go where they want, unchaperoned, never giving it a thought. But if I had been your elder brother," his voice dropped in timbre, "I wouldn't have allowed you to step foot on Italian soil without proper supervision. Having said that, I suggest we go inside. I find that I am in need of sustenance.''

On legs as insubstantial as jelly, she entered the restaurant with him. Her ears picked up the background music of Rossini, the famous composer whose ancestral home of Pesaro was located in the Marches.

After they were seated, Luke helped her translate the menu. When their orders were taken, he excused himself. She decided to use the time to visit the powder room.

They met back at the table five minutes later. As if reading her mind he said, ''I made a phone call to Luciana who sounded disappointed she wouldn't be able to do your hair after all. No doubt she is on the line with Giovanni this minute, alerting him to the change in plans.''

Gaby's voice was hesitant. ''M-maybe we ought to call him and explain what we're doing.''

''The dye has been cast,'' he murmured, sounding vaguely impatient. ''Let's enjoy our meal.''

On that succinct note they put personal worries aside while she was treated to Italian cuisine at its finest. Along with the pasta and rabbit, they ate succulent melon wrapped in prosciutto, and a nutty whole-wheat bread with a *cru* poured over the top made from the olives of just one hillside of the region.

As if that weren't enough, Luke introduced her to a lightly astringent white wine he preferred called *Verdicchio*. To please him, she drank some during the delicious meal, then allowed him to fill her glass again while she accompanied him and the voluble owner inside the villa.

The man was obviously honored by the presence of an illustrious member of the Provere family. He kept smiling at Gaby and insisted on showing her his private collection of an irreplaceable set of hand-painted *maiolica*, a china with the famous blue-and-yellow decoration made around Urbino during the late Renaissance.

The owner would have taken them on a tour of the entire villa if Luke hadn't indicated they were on a deadline and must be on their way. The man walked them to their car, his goodbyes effusive. Luke was probably used to a surfeit of that kind of preferential treatment, but it was a new experience for Gaby who was more or less floating by now.

Being with Luke felt too good, too natural. When he helped her into the car, she didn't pull away at the touch of his hand on her arm. In truth, she welcomed the burning sensation igniting her body. If he hadn't moved to shut the door, she would have rested against him.

Not used to drinking anything alcoholic, the wine had blurred the sharp edges of reality. She had wandered into a dangerous corridor of contentment, willing to follow wherever he led.

For a brief moment, she had the strongest conviction that if she'd turned in his arms just now and pressed her mouth to his, he wouldn't have found the strength to push her away.

Once on the road however, Luke seemed to have removed himself emotionally from her. Deep in his own thoughts, he concentrated on his driving, not bothering to make conversation.

Though she might be feeling the effects of too much wine, he didn't appear to be suffering from the same problem. Ashamed she felt so out of control and unable to suppress her overflowing emotions, she closed her eyes to blot him from her vision. But she hadn't counted on the rich food and lack of sleep the night before to conspire against her so completely.

Her lids grew heavy. She couldn't open them again and at some point oblivion took over. She didn't waken until she discovered them parked outside the small church in Loretello, a wheat-colored brick edifice which seemed to grow organically from the hillside. Earlier, Luke had stopped in Arcevia to make inquiries and she'd never even stirred.

"W-what did you learn?" she asked, smoothing the hair out of her face. Luke's silent scrutiny confused her, making it difficult to think. She was embarrassed to have slept so long.

One black brow dipped in concern. "Not a great deal, I'm afraid. Your great-grandmother's family did not own land in Loretello. They must have moved into the area, farmed someone else's plot of ground, then moved on. There are no Trussardis listed in the birth or death records."

Surprised at the depth of her disappointment, she turned her head away. "It's possible my great-grandmother's memory was faulty and we've been led on a wild-goose chase. I—I appreciate all your help, Luke. You've gone out of your way for nothing.''

''All is not lost,'' he reminded her in a voice of inherent authority. ''We'll visit the church and consult the parish records. Sometimes a detail is overlooked when copies are made for the conservatory archives.''

Gaby shook her head. ''They won't turn up anything, and I don't want to put you to further trouble.''

She heard a muttered imprecation which could have meant any number of things before he levered himself from the car. She scrambled out her door to accompany him, not wanting to incur any more of his displeasure when he'd been trying so hard to help her.

The Medieval facade gave way to an ornate interior and shrine. At the back pew she watched Luke cross himself, reminding her as nothing else could do, that in less than a month, the walls of a church would be his home for the duration of his life.

Her heart felt a sharp, stabbing pain as she, too, made the sign of the cross. Unaware of her turmoil, he asked her to wait while he searched for someone to assist them. Seemingly at home in this sanctuary, he disappeared through a side door.

In agony of spirit, Gaby closed her eyes and prayed for release from the invisible cords binding her to him. She begged for help in forgetting him once she left Italy, begged for peace to come into her heart. Otherwise she'd continue to mourn him, and her whole life would be an utter waste.

"Gabriella?" She heard her name in a tortured whisper. She knew he was worried about Giovanni, but wondered if there wasn't something else burdening him, adding to his turmoil.

Brushing at the moisture on her dark lashes, she stood from a kneeling position, hoping he couldn't tell she'd been crying.

"I expected to talk to the local cure, but he's out visiting. Fortunately the caretaker is on hand. He's willing to let us scan the records in the office."

Only Luke's prominent name and vocation could have induced the groundskeeper to open up such valuable records to a stranger, a foreigner no less. Her debt to Giovanni's brother had grown beyond her ability to repay.

Keeping her head lowered, she turned and followed him to the small anteroom which served as an office with a desk, chairs and several floor-to-ceiling bookcases encased in glass.

She smiled at the wizened caretaker and thanked him in Italian for his kindness. He bowed politely and undid the lock on one of the bookcases. After putting a large tome on the tabletop, he left them alone and shut the door.

Luke indicated she should sit next to him and pushed the ancient-looking record in front of her. "According to what you've told me, your great-grandmother was born somewhere around 1883. Since the earliest she might have met her future husband would be at age fifteen, we can assume she was living here at the turn of the century."

Trying to cover up the trembling his warmth and nearness evoked, she opened the cover.

Luke translated in a low, mellow voice. It resonated to her insides. "This lists a church census covering some births, christenings and baptisms from the years 1834 to 1908. There's a note indicating that a fire in 1900 destroyed part of the record."

"Just the year we're looking for," she lamented.

"Don't jump to conclusions. Let's start with 1885 and move forward."

Throughout the book there were scorch marks, some too brown to read the names entered in ornate cursive handwriting. Gaby came to the portion Luke suggested and ran a nervous finger down the neat rows of names.

Dozens of the same appellation appeared because whole extended families had lived in the area. They turned page after stained-torn page. It became evident that there were no Trussardis listed anywhere.

The handwriting taught in the American public schools didn't resemble European penmanship dating back a century. Most of the time she couldn't tell the difference between a capital J, F, G, I or T.

But Luke, who studied each entry with absolute concentration, had no such problem. For him to spend this kind of time helping her research a name that meant nothing to him, made her love for him that much stronger and binding.

As the pendulum of the antique wall clock swung back and forth marking the passage of time, she realized that she'd probably never know about her namesake's origins.

"Luke—" She touched his arm gently. His eyes swiveled to hers in puzzled query, and she removed her hand. "It's no use."

"Maybe," he murmured. "Maybe not. Will you hand me that large magnifying glass hanging on the peg next to the bookcase?"

"Yes. Of course." She got up and reached for it, then gave it to him. "Have you found something?"

"I'm not sure. There are about ten pages badly stained, but I can just make out some of the names." He stood up and went over to the window to take advantage of what little light it afforded.

For once Gaby had an excuse to feast her eyes on him. Right now she could easily imagine him in robes of an important holy office. There was a magnificence about his physical presence as well as a nobility of character that shone through. He would make his mark in the church.

Yet Gaby had glimpsed a sensuous side to his nature. Today there'd been brief moments of ecstasy when she'd caught sight of his rare smile and heard his full-bodied laughter. And there'd been other times when the hunger in his eyes had turned her body molten. She couldn't have imagined those looks, could she?

That's what was tormenting her now...the possibility that she'd wanted him so much, she'd fooled herself into believing her presence affected him in a similar fashion.

"*Santa Maria!*" she heard him mutter, jerking her from her inner torment. With her heart thudding, she rose to her feet.

"Luke—"

"The date at the top of the page is missing. But according to the ones I can read, we know it has to be sometime between 1882 and 1885. It appears that a Vittore Ridolfi and wife, Amalia, had an infant, Gabriella, christened."

His black eyes flashed with a strange light. "This is the only Gabriella I've come across in any of the records at Arcevia or here. How strange that there is no birth date on her when the Ridolfi name is quite prolific in this region." He sounded far away.

Gaby started to get chills of excitement. "What are you thinking?"

His gaze encompassed her flushed face. "There is no evidence that this couple had children born to them. It's possible they took someone else's daughter to raise."

Her thoughts raced. "You mean she might have been an unwanted pregnancy and was either abandoned by her real mother or given up for adoption."

A frown line etched his dark brow. "There could be many circumstances we're not aware of. Perhaps the natural parents were killed while in the area, leaving the child orphaned. Or the Ridolfis might have been so anxious to have a baby, it's possible they traveled further afield to find one needing a home. It wasn't uncommon for a family with too many mouths to feed to sell a daughter."

A horrible reality Gaby hated to think about. "But if they raised her as their own, why didn't she take on their name instead of calling herself Trussardi?"

"Maybe one of the parents couldn't accept the child wholeheartedly and reminded her she wasn't their blood."

"It might explain why she ran off with my great-grandfather at the first opportunity."

Luke put the book and magnifying glass back on the table. "Whatever the explanation, we now have a name and something to go on. I want to talk to the caretaker. He must be in his seventies. If there are any present day Ridolfis living in Loretello, he'll know of them."

Unbelievably, Luke seemed as caught up in the excitement of solving this mystery as she was. Before they left the church, the caretaker had given them directions to the farm of one Carlo Ridolfi.

Once they were in the car, however, guilt assailed her. "Luke, I'm more grateful for your help than you'll ever know. As far as I'm concerned, it's a miracle you came across a name that could have been my relative. It's enough to have learned this much, b-but we should be getting back to Urbino." Her voice caught.

When he didn't say anything, she bent her head. "I'm leaving early in the morning and still have things to do." Being in his company like this was tearing her apart.

At her words, an almost ominous stillness pervaded the atmosphere. "You're not going anywhere until we find what we came for."

Shaken, she murmured, "But that might not be possible."

"We'll see," was all he would concede, sending a thrill of alarm through her body.

CHAPTER SIX

BY THE time they found the Ridolfi farm on the outskirts of Loretello, the late afternoon sun had lost a little of its heat. Luke shut off the air conditioner and lowered the windows so they could breathe the luscious scent coming from the vineyards lining the road.

The tile-roofed farmhouse rested on a hillside surrounded by well-tended crops of vegetables planted in perfect lines. A middle-aged farmer working down one of the rows heard their car and waved.

After a brief exchange which she couldn't follow, Luke translated. Apparently the man named Lorenzo said they would find his father, Carlo, over the other side of the hill tying vines.

Once more the car followed the meandering lane until they arrived at another stretch of vineyard. Here they came upon the short, leather-faced family patriarch in dark beret and white shirt sleeves. He looked at least eighty years old, yet worked with the speed of his son.

Luke got out of the car and walked over to him. For the next ten minutes Gaby stayed put, watching and listening in rapt attention as the two men conversed back and forth, using their hands to demonstrate everything they were saying. A long time ago she decided that if you tied an Italian's hands, he wouldn't be able to talk at all.

When she saw Luke unexpectedly put a hand on the old man's shoulder and shake the other one in a firm grip, her heart rate accelerated because she had a feeling he'd learned something important.

Luke's black eyes held a triumphant gleam as the two men walked toward the car. The old farmer's mouth broke into a broad smile when Luke introduced her as Gabriella.

"What have you found out?" she cried, hardly able to contain her excitement.

"Carlo's great uncle once removed was Vittore Ridolfi. Apparently Vittore was the outcast of the Ridolfi clan who farmed a piece of family property in the next valley.

"The story goes that as a young man, he had a bit of a wild streak and went to Rome for a fortnight. When he returned, he brought back a young woman who'd already had a baby by another man."

"Amalia! Then that means my great-grandmother might have been born in or around Rome."

Luke nodded. "Yes. He insisted on marrying her, but the family refused to recognize the child. When the girl, Gabriella, grew up, she ran off with an American and was never seen again. It broke the mother's heart. They died childless."

"Oh—" Gaby's eyes smarted painfully. "How sad for them when my great-grandmother was so happy in her own marriage."

Luke expelled a breath. "Carlo says the girl was known to have her mother's red hair. She was also reputed to be a great beauty, just like you." His voice sounded thick.

She knew he was only passing on the other man's compliment, but his tone made it so personal, her body trembled.

As if Carlo understood what was going on, he nodded and pointed to her hair. More Italian poured out of him. When he finished talking, a slow smile broke a corner of Luke's mouth, dazzling her with his masculine beauty.

"Carlo is delighted to learn that you are her great-granddaughter. One day soon he would like to gather the family for a picnic to meet you and hear all the details. There are twenty-five to thirty relatives still living in the environs."

She swallowed hard. "Tell him I would love that, but since I'm leaving in the morning, it's impossible."

Lines slowly marred his handsome features before he began another translation. The old man listened with a frown.

"He says you must come back."

She didn't dare meet the fierce intensity of Luke's gaze. "Maybe one day." It was a struggle to keep her emotions contained. "Would you ask him if I could see the place where she was raised?"

More conversation ensued. "He says the original shell of the farmhouse is still standing, but nowadays the inside is used for storage by one of his cousins. He has given you permission to walk around and do whatever you like for as long as you like. I'll take you there now."

With tears trickling from her eyes, Gaby thrust her hand out the window to shake Carlo's hand. To her surprise, he leaned forward, cupped her face and kissed both cheeks.

"Squisita, signorina—" he murmured over and over again amid a volley of other words she didn't understand. When he finally let her go, she sat back in the seat, blushing outrageously from his spontaneous display of affection.

"You've made a real conquest," Luke inserted wryly under his breath as he started the engine and they drove off. "He gave me his address. I told him you would keep in touch."

"T-thank you," she whispered, overcome with such deep love for Luke, she couldn't find the words. To hide her feelings, she leaned her head out the window once more to wave at Carlo.

"Arrivederci!" he called after her, using the familiar form of the word goodbye, a word reserved for family and close friends only. It warmed her heart. She shouted the same word back to him and kept waving until they descended the next hill and she couldn't see him anymore.

Settling back again, she let out a delighted cry to see another quaint farmhouse in the distance, sitting on a small knoll. Lush meadows interspersed with manicured cherry orchards spread to its foundation like the spokes of a wheel to its center.

She was looking at the playground of her great-grandmother. It was too perfect to be real.

"T-this is one of the most thrilling moments of my life." Her voice shook. "I owe it all to you."

There were tears in her voice and eyes. "How will I ever be able to thank you properly?"

She heard his sharp intake of breath. "If you could see the look on your face, you'd know that you already have."

He pulled to the side of the road. When he suggested they go for a walk, she was already out of the car, running toward the farmhouse.

The slanting rays of the sun cast long shadows as she made her way through the orchard. She remembered her great-grandmother talking about climbing trees, playing with her doll in the top branches.

Gaby noted that cherry trees were absolutely wonderful for climbing. Shaped like U-joints, the branches which grew low on the trunk made it a simple matter to attain one level, then another.

Near the farmhouse she saw one large, sturdy tree whose cherries hadn't been picked on top. Perhaps it was a favorite of her great-grandmother's. Unable to resist, Gaby left her purse in the grass and started climbing. Three-quarters of the way up she found a bunch of dark red fruit and ate the cherries right off their stems. "Hmm... These taste like ambrosia."

Depositing the pips in her palm, then tossing them in the opposite direction, she plucked another spray. "Here—" she called to Luke, her mouth half full of sweet, ripe cherries. "These are for you."

She dangled the bunch so he'd be sure to spot it. An imp of mischief prompted her to taunt, "If you want them, you'll have to come and get them."

He wouldn't accept the challenge, of course, but she hadn't been able to resist throwing it out. Somewhere eight to ten feet below the leaves, he was standing there waiting for her to come down.

A particularly gorgeous bunch of cherries lured her another foot higher. As she grabbed for it, she disturbed an enormous black and yellow queen bee whose buzz sounded like a small motor. She screamed in fright and suddenly the entire tree shook as Luke made it up the trunk in record time.

"What's wrong?" he demanded, his dark head pushing through the leaves.

"A queen bee!" she screamed again as it tried to land on her hair. Ill with fright, she jerked to get out of harm's way and almost lost her footing.

"It's after you, all right," he muttered. "Stay perfectly still."

Trusting in him completely, she willed herself not to move, but the hideous whirring noise made her heart thud with sickening irregularity.

With a calm she could scarcely fathom, Luke broke off a good-size shoot of leaves and thrust the huge insect from her hair with all his force. A few strands were pulled from her scalp but she didn't feel them.

All she knew was an overwhelming sense of relief as she watched the bee sail through the air in a great arc, stunned by the whack Luke had given it. Her body shaking out of control, she hurtled herself into Luke's arms.

He crushed her against his chest. "That bee won't be going anywhere for a while," he assured her in a low, soothing tone, his face buried in her hair.

"Thank God," she cried, burrowing into the warmth of his neck where she could feel a strong pulse beating frantically. "I'm allergic to bee stings."

He bit out a smothered epithet. "Whatever possessed you to climb this tree?"

His hands moved over her back, sending tiny currents of electricity through her throbbing body. "I don't know. I—I was so happy to have found her home I didn't stop to think, and the cherries looked so tempting."

He lifted his head, his black eyes doing a lightning-fast appraisal of her red-stained mouth. "There's cherry juice everywhere. No wonder the bee came after you." His voice sounded slurred.

Caught in a V of the tree, Gaby became conscious that her body was molded to the hard length of his. With no space separating them, she could feel the pounding of his heart, the tremors that shook his powerful frame.

"*Mio Dio!*" he vented a violent imprecation. "Talk about temptation…that heart-shaped mouth would drive a saint to commit the unforgivable." Groaning in self-denigration he closed his mouth over hers, cutting off any possibility of escape.

After aching so long for this intimacy, Gaby was thankful to be trapped against his hard body with no place to go except to merge with him.

She knew this was a momentary aberration on his part. When he had satiated the desire which had temporarily flared out of control because they were wedged together, he'd let her go, regretting his weakness. They would return to Urbino and their separate lives, never to know this kind of exultation again.

But for Gaby, this was the supreme moment of her life. The man she wanted more than life itself was holding her, kissing her with breathtaking urgency. This moment would have to last her forever.

On a little moan of desperation she surrendered herself, denying him nothing, offering him everything in a kiss that blotted out time, space, conscience...

What she couldn't say in words, she said with her lips, her hands. She was starving for him and would gorge herself on his mouth for as long as he allowed this mindless ecstasy to continue.

Gaby had so little experience with men, she had no idea what she was doing. Right now she was driven by sheer, primitive, female instinct. The man she wanted was about to disappear from her life, never to be seen again. Until he thrust her away from him, she would show him just exactly what he meant to her.

"Gabriella—" he groaned her name as if it had been ripped out of him, his hands possessive and exploring. When she felt his mouth against the pale, scented skin of her neck, coherent thought ceased. She yielded so completely to his demands, they moved as one living entity.

The black hair she'd longed to touch filled her hands. Intoxicated by his enticing male scent, her mouth followed where her fingers trailed, pressing feverish kisses to his throat, ears and eyes.

Blinded by passion, her lips memorized the lines and angles of his face, the sensuous curve of his compelling mouth. Wild with desire, she couldn't get enough of him.

In such a euphoric state, she suffered shock when he suddenly wrenched her forearms from around his neck, breaking their kiss so abruptly, she cried his name out of deprivation, her blue eyes hurt and uncomprehending.

"For the love of God, Gabriella—" She heard his tortured whisper before he started cursing savagely in his native tongue. "You will descend the tree first, *per favore*. Now!" he demanded when she hesitated.

Trembling from the force of her emotions, Gaby had to make herself do his bidding, but the going down was almost an impossibility. She was forced to cling to each branch for a minute while her body swayed, still giddy from reaction to his touch.

Here and there her skirt caught on a twig, lifting it thigh-high as her shapely leg searched for another foothold. When she realized that this was the reason Luke had insisted she go ahead of him, her face reddened in embarrassment.

By the time she'd reached the ground, total recall of the uninhibited way she'd responded to him in the treetop turned the upper half of her body scarlet.

Good heavens, what a trembling, love-crazed mess she was! If either of the Ridolfis could see her now, they'd know exactly what she'd been doing. Her hair was a mop of dishevelment from Luke's questing hands and mouth. There were traces of lipstick and cherry stains on her white top.

To her consternation, her heart refused to resume its normal beat rate. She was breathing as if she'd just run a marathon, and her lips were swollen and tender from the explosion of passion Luke had unleashed.

Behind her she felt him jump to the ground. "I'll meet you at the car," was all he deigned to say in a gravelly tone before leaving her on her own.

Startled, she turned to watch him, a dark, lean figure whose long, swift strides emphasized emotional as well as physical distancing from her.

She should have been ashamed of her wanton behavior. But how could she be when those moments in his arms had been so perfect? There was no denying he'd been an equal partner in the experience, that he'd been as witless as she during that fusion of mouths and bodies and souls.

At least *her* soul was involved, her heart cried in agony. According to Giovanni, Luke's soul had been reserved for God.

She wasn't so naive about men that she didn't know even a man of the cloth could be tempted to enjoy lovemaking in the purely physical sense without his emotions becoming involved. Given her out-of-control response, he'd succumbed to what she'd blatantly offered because Luke had his human side, too. Only the fact that they were in a tree prevented the inevitable from happening. But the experience hadn't changed his life out of all recognition. He'd been able to walk away from her without once looking back.

She, on the other hand, still ached from longings he'd aroused but would never assuage. What really terrified her was that she might remain in this untenable condition for the rest of her life.

For the moment her only resource was to take a little time to compose herself before she returned to the car. She had her pride and wouldn't allow him to see what he'd done to her.

Reaching for her purse, she tidied herself as best she could with her hairbrush and lipstick, then pulled out her instamatic camera. For the next few minutes she snapped various views of the farmhouse and orchard.

To her chagrin, she had a feeling every picture would be blurry because she was shaking so hard. Her family might be overjoyed with the visual evidence of her great-grandmother's home, but they'd want an explanation for her less than expert photographic prowess.

No one could ever know about this interlude with Luke. She would have to twist the truth and tell her family that a queen bee had been chasing her.

But that was the least of her worries. Right now she needed to deal with a much bigger problem. How was she going to face Luke who'd been sitting in the Maserati for a good fifteen minutes, no doubt regretting his momentary insanity and impatient to be gone.

It was late. Twilight had fast turned into evening. It stole over the colorful landscape, deepening the shadows, magnifying the serenity a hundredfold.

She should never have climbed that tree. While they'd been locked together, she'd lost cognizance of her world, ignoring the reality of the situation. Deep inside, Gaby had known there'd be a price to pay for tasting forbidden fruit. She just hadn't realized how excruciating the pain would be. It was like tearing her heart out to leave this paradise where she'd experienced rapture.

More time was lost as she fought to keep her tears at bay, then made her way through the fragrant orchard toward the car.

The low, purring sound of the motor told her how anxious Luke was to return to Urbino. With yet another reason to feel guilty, she climbed in the passenger side. The second she shut the door, a fluid motion of his hand put the car into gear and they were off.

On their way to the main road, she saw Carlo's lighted farmhouse out of the periphery. But she didn't dare look in that direction or she'd see Luke's forbidding countenance.

It didn't seem possible that she'd known a passion beyond belief in the arms of this remote, taciturn stranger piloting the car as if it had wings.

Obviously guilt was eating him alive. Gaby knew the feeling. They'd betrayed Giovanni, which was bad enough. But in Luke's own mind, he'd done something much worse this close to being professed. She couldn't let him take all the blame.

"L-Luke?" she whispered tentatively.

"If you don't mind, *signorina*, I prefer not to talk about what happened," came the wintry voice she dreaded. "You found the home of your namesake. Let that be the memory you take back to Nevada."

Intense anger intruded on her pain. His hurtful dismissal of something as earthshaking and intimate as what they had shared at the farm, blinded her to caution.

With eyes burning like hot blue coals, she flung her head around, causing the hair to swish against her hot cheek. "Is that the memory you plan to take back to the Vatican, Father Luca?" Her question rang throughout the tension-filled interior.

By the time she felt enough remorse to wish she could recall it, he'd pulled to the side of the road and shut off the engine.

With his right hand still on the wheel, he turned his head in her direction. His eyes were black slits of light. "How long have you known?" he demanded thickly.

She bit the inside of her lower lip. "Giovanni told me when he dropped me off at the *pensione* last night."

He muttered something terrifyingly unintelligible before ejecting himself from the car. The slam of the door gave eloquent testimony of his state of mind. She had the gut feeling few people, if any, had ever seen Luca Provere this out of control.

In other circumstances she might have congratulated herself, even rejoiced that she was the reason for his uncharacteristic behavior. But her conscience forbade her to feel anything but shame for the eagerness with which she'd played her part in that tree. Her feverish abandon had probably sent Luke into shock and he was still trying to recover.

When she thought she couldn't stand to be alone with her tortured thoughts any longer, the driver's door opened. Headlights of a passing car illuminated Luke's grimaced features before he climbed inside and shut it again. She held her breath until he spoke.

"We have to talk," his voice rasped, "but not on this road where someone will stop because they have the mistaken notion my car has broken down."

The powerful engine roared to life. She heard the tires squeal as he drove onto the pavement.

A nervous shiver invaded her body. "The alley behind the *pensione* is private. W-we could talk there," she stammered uncertainly.

The silence following her suggestion made Gaby realize she'd said the wrong thing. He probably thought she was hinting to be alone with him so they could continue what had gone on in the cherry tree.

"The traffic is heavier than usual tonight." He ignored her suggestion. "We won't reach Urbino in time to do anything but drive to the hospital. As it is, we'll probably have to waken Giovanni so you can say your goodbyes."

The bleakness of his tone caused her eyes to close tightly. She'd forgotten all about Giovanni.

"I can't go there looking like this!" She panicked. "He'll know that we—that I—" Her voice caught. She couldn't finish what she was trying to say.

Luke raked an unsteady hand through his dark hair. "He'll know I couldn't keep my hands off you," he growled. "*Per Dio!*" came another soul-wrenching sound. "My little brother will see that I couldn't be trusted to do him the only favor he has ever asked of me." His voice shook with self-loathing.

She caught at the straps of her purse. "You're not to blame," she asserted forcefully. "I'm the one who is ashamed. I—I knew you were on the verge of taking holy vows, but it didn't stop me from—" All the air seemed to leave her lungs and she struggled for breath.

"The point is," she went on raggedly, "I'm as wretched as my great-grandmother. Her selfish desires for a man caused her to run away with him. She never stopped to consider the trail of broken hearts she left behind.

"The only difference here is—" Gaby paused to swallow. "We've done nothing so serious tha—"

"*Basta*!" He silenced her. "If we had made it as far as the inside of the farmhouse, we would still be in there and probably not venture outside again until someone disturbed us."

He was speaking the truth, which was why she couldn't say anything. The images his words conjured up sent delicious chills through her trembling body.

His black eyes bored into her. "Even in your naïveté, you realize that I almost made love to you."

"Yes." He dragged the word out of her.

"*Mio Dio*," he raged. "Do you think it makes me proud to admit that you reduced me to the level of an adolescent schoolboy hungry for his first experience with a woman? One look at those gorgeous legs disappearing up the trunk of that tree and every thought but one went out of my head."

She stared at her hands. "Please don't crucify yourself, Luke. I—I'm to blame for everything that has happened."

A strange sound escaped his throat. "What exactly does that mean?"

Girding up her courage, she said, "Giovanni told me you haven't been home for a whole year, that you've been closeted with other men of the priesthood. My father has always taught me that a woman has the power to tempt a man."

Bending her head, she murmured, "I should never have climbed that tree. I completely forgot I was wearing a skirt. It wasn't fair to you."

A bitterly angry laugh broke from him. "Your willingness to take my sin upon your head is nothing short of amazing. After your self-sacrificing speech, I hate to disillusion you, but the truth is, I've been lusting after you since the moment Giovanni introduced us."

CHAPTER SEVEN

LUKE'S bald admission was so unexpected, Gaby had no conception of where to go from here. Her instincts about him hadn't been wrong. Their desire for each other had been a mutual thing. But now reality had asserted itself.

She should be thanking God that they hadn't gone inside the farmhouse. To have known the joy of his possession and then watch him go back to Rome would have destroyed her completely. As it was, returning to Nevada meant facing a horrendous adjustment she didn't have the strength to contemplate.

Mired in his own black thoughts, the man at her side remained unbearably silent for the rest of the drive back to Urbino.

"W-what will we say to Giovanni?" she finally ventured when he pulled into the casualty parking lot an hour later.

He brought the car to a stop and turned off the motor. "We'll tell him you preferred doing genealogy to going to the ball."

"But—"

"It's eleven-fifteen," he cut in on her tersely. "There's no time for discussion. By now Giovanni will have been put in a private room. We'll get that information first. Come."

112

He didn't make a pretense of helping her from the car, but now she knew the reason why. He didn't trust himself alone with her. Under other circumstances she would have been elated at his astonishing confession.

But he was no ordinary man. He had a calling, a destiny. Since he'd been so honest with her, she had no business diverting him from his chosen path, no matter how unintentional her behavior.

As she followed him inside the emergency room, she made a promise to herself. Until they said goodbye, she'd do everything in her power to help them both forget what had transpired at Loretello.

She stood at the end of the main desk while he made inquiries, noting that only one cubicle was in use. Everything was much quieter tonight.

Try as she might not to look, her eyes seemed to have a will of their own and she found herself staring through veiled lashes at the man who'd kissed her into oblivion earlier in the day. He was in deep discussion with one of the nurses and appeared perplexed. Suddenly his jet black gaze found Gaby and he started toward her.

"Giovanni is no longer in the hospital." He ran a finger around the back of his collar in obvious puzzlement. "It seems he insisted on recovering at home, so his doctor released him. My mother sent a car."

"That's wonderful!" Gaby cried. The news that he was so much better brought her tremendous relief, particularly since she had no idea how she would have stood up to Giovanni's scrutiny. Very little passed by him unnoticed.

"Now you can leave for Rome in the morning with no worries," she said in a deceptively bright voice, determined to carry out her charade. "I hate to ask this last favor, but would you mind running me to the *pensione* on your way home?"

Luke's dark head reeled back as if she'd just struck him. His features looked chiseled. "You haven't said goodbye to him yet," came the solemn pronouncement.

She started to feel uneasy. "I—I realize that— but visiting him at the castle at this late hour is out of the question." She looked away from him. "Your mother would never approve, not when Giovanni and I aren't engaged to be married."

The truth of her words must have reached him because there was no swift retort. The tension was back, much worse than before. He was standing too close.

The male scent of his warm skin, the trace of fragrance from the soap he'd used that morning, combined to remind her of things she shouldn't be thinking about, like the taste and feel of his mouth, the way it had devoured hers, the incredible things it had done to her before he'd pushed her away.

A burning crept into her face and she gulped. "I—I have to be in front of the university at five forty-five in the morning to board my bus. I'll call him en route and say a final goodbye over the phone."

Unable to take any more of this, Gaby fled the emergency room and hurried out to the car ahead of him. Once ensconced in the Maserati, she rummaged in her purse for her camera while Luke took his place behind the wheel and started up the engine.

In the short time it took them to reach the outskirts of town, she wound the film and removed it from the camera, anything to keep her hands and thoughts occupied.

"Y-you can just let me off in front," she said jerkily when he turned onto the narrow street of the place she'd called home for the last six weeks.

The knuckles of his hand looked a pinched white as he wove between the parked cars to the entrance. For a moment she feared he would ignore her suggestion and drive around to the back alley.

The feelings running rampant inside her were too explosive for her to ever be alone with him again. Before he applied his brakes, she had the door open. A smothered epithet from his side of the car didn't discourage her from jumping out on the bricked street the second he slowed down.

Gaby heard her name called but she didn't pause. Instead, she shut the door behind her, then ran around the back of his car to the entrance of the *pensione*.

Ten fragile feet separated them. She refused to meet his scorching gaze.

"Thank you for all you did for me today." She fought for breath. "My family and I will forever be in your debt. Give my love to Giovanni. Tell him I'll be in touch with him soon." She clung to the handle of the door. "God bless you, Luke." Her voice cracked before she disappeared through the doors.

The minute she reached her room, she collapsed on the bed in abject despair. Alone at last, she didn't have to hold back the tears. It was like a dam had burst.

Up to now, Gaby had led a very happy life. Like everyone else, she'd experienced moments of sadness and had shed tears. But she'd never known this kind of pain before. The mattress shook with her heart-wrenching sobs. Afraid the girls on either side of her room might hear, she attempted to stifle the sounds with her pillow.

The night seemed endless. Around four in the morning, she got up from the bed so puffy-eyed, no more tears could creep out her lids.

Quietly, she tiptoed down the hall to the bathroom for a shower. One look in the mirror while she was brushing her teeth and she recoiled from the ghostly looking apparition staring back at her. Anyone seeing her right now would think she was a witch.

After shampooing her hair, she stood under the tepid water, praying the rinse would wash away her memories of Luke along with the suds. But nothing could do that. Not even if she lived to be a hundred.

While her hair was still damp, she formed it into one long braid, then put on a clean pair of comfortable, well-worn Levi's and cotton blouse for the bus trip to Belgium. Twelve hours from now she'd be hundreds of miles from here. From Luke . . .

More tears started, burning her eyes. She refused to give in to them and marched out of the bathroom to her room. Within twenty minutes everything was packed in her two pieces of luggage.

The used linen she put in a laundry bag by the door for the maids. One short trip to Celeste's room where she slid a note with her address under the door, and she was ready to go.

Returning to her room, she looked around a last time, making sure she hadn't left anything behind.

Who would have dreamed that two days before her fabulous trip to Italy came to an end, all her joy would turn to debilitating pain?

It was so early, she assumed most of the girls were still asleep when she crept past the empty dining hall to the front door of the *pensione*. The thought of having to talk to anyone was anathema to her. So was food.

Normally she walked to the university every day. But with two heavy suitcases in hand, she'd never make it. This morning she planned to wait for the local bus which stopped at the end of her street and drove past the university as part of its scheduled run.

All the Americans attending Urbino university from around the U.S. would be boarding their tour bus within the hour. Arriving early at the meeting place in the piazza would ensure her a window seat up front, away from the gregarious party types.

If possible, she would try to save a couple of seats for her friends, Joan and Lorraine, who would be getting on in Florence. Their company would make the rest of her trip bearable.

After giving one last fond look around the interior of her bed and breakfast situation, she repressed the sob in her throat, stepped outside and quietly shut the door behind her.

"I'll help you with those." A low, familiar masculine voice broke the stillness, causing her to gasp.

Gaby whirled around, gaping at Luke incredulously as he reached for her cases and stowed them in the Maserati. In a slate blue silk shirt and dark trousers, he looked particularly stunning, robbing her of the little breath she had left.

"What are you doing here?" Her cry of alarm came out like an accusation, but she couldn't help it. Throughout the long night she'd fought an endless battle with pain. Now he was back, tearing her to shreds all over again.

His encompassing black glance swept over her, reducing her limbs to liquid. "Giovanni has disappeared," came the tight-lipped response.

"*Disappeared*?" She could never have anticipated such a turn of events.

In a state of absolute shock, she didn't remonstrate when Luke assisted her into the passenger seat. He shut the door and came around to start up the car. This close to him she noticed new worry lines etched on his striking features. He didn't look as if he'd had any sleep, either.

"Luke—" She called his name, suddenly remembering. "My bus! It's—"

"*Basta, Gabriella*!" he interrupted as if he couldn't take much more, then muttered something definitely unpleasant in Italian. She couldn't possibly translate the string of expletives, but it showed the depth of his turmoil.

"Right now we must deal with an emergency. Naturally I will make other arrangements for you to fly to Nevada. When we arrive at the palazzo, I will inform the tour company of your change in plans."

She moaned. Another delay. Another heartache. "W-when did you discover him missing?" By now they'd reached the end of the narrow street and had entered the mainstream of traffic.

"Luciana had instructions to keep an eye on him during the night. Sometime between three and four this morning, he left his room and hasn't been seen since. My mother is beside herself. She asked that I bring you to the palazzo."

His comments put new fear in her heart. "You mean you have no idea where he is?"

"None at all," came the grim rejoinder. "She was hoping that you might know something the rest of us do not." His clipped words underlined the stress he was dealing with.

She bowed her head. "I don't know any more than you do."

"You swear you're telling the truth?" he demanded like someone who'd reached the limit of his tolerance.

Hurt by his question, she turned on him. "Do you honestly think I would lie to you after— after—" She couldn't finish the rest and felt the shudder that passed through his body.

"No, I didn't think that." The words sounded dragged out of him. "*Per Dio*, this is a complication I would never have imagined."

To her consternation, another car almost crashed into them. Only Luke's competence at the wheel prevented them from having an accident.

"When you returned to the palazzo last night, d-did you tell him we went to Loretello?" she ventured in a tremulous voice.

"I would have," he grated, "but when I entered his room, he was asleep. I preferred not to disturb him."

Another wave of guilt engulfed her. "Do you think he found out we didn't go to the ball, and he was upset about it?"

"I've been asking myself that same question, but it hardly matters now. He's nowhere to be found." His voice echoed her own growing panic over his disappearance.

"Does your mother know we were together most of yesterday and last night?"

"Yes," was all he condescended to say until they reached the covered archway at the rear of the ducal estate. A male servant appeared on the steps. Upon Luke's instructions, the older man retrieved her bags from the car and took them inside.

Gaby had never thought to see the palazzo again, let alone the inside of the red and white room. Yet that was where Luke's mother was waiting for them, her face a picture of anguish.

The second they stepped foot inside the paneled doors, she got to her feet and rushed over to Gaby, reaching for her hands.

"Ah, Signorina Holt. Thank you for coming," she emoted softly, pulling Gaby down on the tapestry-covered love seat with her.

The older woman's reception was so different from the night of the dinner, Gaby could scarcely credit this was the same person.

Luke stood a few feet away from them, his hand rubbing the back of his bronzed neck in contemplation. Gaby couldn't forget what he'd told her, that his mother worshipped Giovanni. Evidently now that he was missing, even Gaby was welcome if she could help solve the mystery of his whereabouts.

"Tell me what has happened to *mio figlio, signorina*. He is still recovering from that horrible accident."

Gaby flashed Luke a signal of distress. His dark gaze swiveled from her to his mother. "I'm afraid Signorina Holt is as perplexed as we are, Mama."

"No—" She shook her head. "I do not believe that. My son intends to marry her, Luca. At the hospital, he refused to see me or talk to me. He has never behaved that way in his life. Only another woman could have that kind of power over him. That woman is *you, signorina*."

"Signora Provere," Gaby began, feeling as if she were drowning, and going under for the third time. "I'm afraid your son has led you to believe something that isn't true. The fact is, Giovanni never asked me to marry him because he knows I'm not in love with him." Her voice shook.

"What are you saying?" His mother's dark brown eyes flashed. "I do not understand. He loves you."

Gaby swallowed hard. "Nevertheless, Giovanni and I are not planning a wedding. We're simply good friends. He invited me here to—to—"

"Mama," Luke intervened. To Gaby's heartfelt relief, he broke into a spate of Italian, explaining the true circumstances of that night. His mother listened with downbent head, her expression changing from grief to shock.

"Is my son correct, *signorina*? You and my Giovanni do not have an understanding?"

"No, *signora*. As I have told you, we are close, more like brother and sister. I haven't seen or heard from him since the night of the accident. If I had any idea where he was, any idea at all, I would tell you."

Because it was the truth, her earnestness must have reached Giovanni's mother. The older woman slowly released Gaby's hands and stared into space through dimmed eyes, looking twenty years older.

Gaby could have wept for the pain Giovanni had caused his family. Why had he done this to them? He'd shrouded his actions in mystery, making it impossible for any of them to function normally.

As if she were in a trance, Signora Provere got up from the couch and looked straight at Gaby. "You've spent the last six weeks with him. Where do you *think* he might be, *signorina*?" she asked in a dull voice.

It was a searching question, requiring a response. Luke's eyes were riveted to her, as well. He, too, was waiting for some kind of clue which would lead them to Giovanni.

Gaby clasped her hands, praying for inspiration. "If he has close friends, I never met any of them, nor did he ever mention their names to me. We spent hours going to museums and galleries, exploring the town. He knows everything about Renaissance art and history."

"That is all?" his mother rasped. "He didn't talk to you about what was going on inside of him?"

"Yes. He told me many things." Gaby stopped pacing. "As you both know, Giovanni's a very spiritual person. He's the kind of man who lives in the world, but isn't of the world, if I'm making sense."

Luke nodded gravely and put a supporting arm around his mother's fragile shoulders. "Go on," he urged, giving Gaby his consent to speak frankly.

"Well, for example, take the other evening when he drove me home from the palace. We had plans to go to the Renaissance ball the next night, so he brought me a jeweled hair piece to wear, and—"

"What hair piece are you talking about?" his mother interrupted, obviously at a loss to explain her son's abnormal behavior.

"Pollaiulo's elaborate pearl headdress masterpiece from our ancestor's private treasury," Luke supplied grimly.

Signora Provere's astonished cry rang throughout the room. She flung her hands in the air. "But that hair piece is priceless and now belongs to the church. It's valued at close to a million dollars."

It was Gaby's turn to be stunned. "I knew it was valuable, but I never dreamed—" Her voice trailed. Now she understood the look Luke had sent

Giovanni's way after opening the bag at the hospital.

"My son asked you to wear it?" His mother's voice came out more like a squeak.

"Yes." Gaby hated to admit it, noting the other woman's complete shock. "You see, Giovanni and I met in the museum while I was looking at it, trying to figure out how Pollaiuolo fashioned it to harmonize with the movement of braids. It was the most beautiful piece of Renaissance jewelry I have ever seen."

When no one spoke, Gaby cleared her throat nervously. "I often wear braids, but couldn't imagine how to arrange it. He got very excited and showed me a fourteenth-century painting of Simonetta Vespucci wearing the exact piece. That way I could see precisely how it should be worn."

"If he did all that for you, then it appears my son was enamored by you from the moment you two met," Signora Provere murmured sadly, but there was no censure in her tone, for which Gaby was grateful.

This gave her the confidence to go on. "H-he was very charming and so easy to talk to. He obviously remembered our conversation that first day in the museum, and insisted I wear the jewelry to the ball.

"But because I knew it was a family treasure, I told him I wouldn't be responsible for keeping it overnight. In fact, I remember telling him that I'd die if anything happened to it while it was in my possession.

"That's when he told me that no earthly treasure was worth dying for. But a sacred love, that was something else again..."

Signora Provere appeared dumbstruck while Luke's brooding gaze wandered over her, his thoughts inscrutable. "Did my brother often confide his innermost secrets to you?" he prodded with surprising tenacity.

"Some of them. I learned right away that his favorite place on earth is inside a church. When we first met, he made me promise to visit Assisi before I left Italy. He told me of a spiritual experience he had while visiting there as a teenager, but asked me not to tell anyone."

"*Mio Dio*—" The ragged oath coming out of Luke sounded agonized.

"I—I'm breaking his confidence by even mentioning it to you, but I'm too concerned about his disappearance to worry about that right now."

"I've never heard of any of this," his mother blurted in bewilderment. "Luca?" She turned to her son, laying her head against his chest. "What is she talking about? Has Giovanni told you of this experience?"

But Luke seemed miles away. His gaze held a strange glitter, exaggerating his pallor. That in turn frightened Gaby.

"Mama—" He unexpectedly put his mother aside. "Please take charge of our guest and offer her every comfort." His black eyes pierced Gaby. "Signorina Holt. You will stay here until my return." The edict fell from his taut lips.

"Luca—where are you going?" his mother asked the question in Gaby's mind, but his exit was so swift, he either didn't hear her, or he was in such a hurry, he chose not to answer. It was like a second death to see him go.

"Something very strange is going on with both my sons. *Santa Maria*! I don't know what to think. Please, my dear. Sit down. I'll ask Luciana to bring us coffee and we will talk. I need to ask your forgiveness for the way I treated you at dinner. As Luca pointed out, I was extremely rude to you and must make amends."

"Please, Signora Provere. There is nothing to forgive. Giovanni led you to believe something that wasn't true and it came as too great a shock."

"That's very charitable of you, *signorina*. I can understand why Giovanni adores you."

Gaby couldn't take much more of this and was growing more and more impatient to be gone.

"Much as I'd love to stay, *signora*, I don't have the time." Girding up her courage, she said, "I— I heard the clock chime on the half hour. My bus is leaving Urbino in a few minutes. If you could ask someone to bring my bags to the foyer and drive me to the university, I can just make it."

Her eyes were dark pinpoints of light. "You heard Luca. He expects you to be here when he gets back."

Gaby's instincts about Luke had been correct. Though he might be forfeiting the title of duke because of his religious affiliation, he was the true heir and natural ruler of the House of Provere. Even his mother deferred to him, but this was one time when Gaby would have to go against his wishes.

"There is no reason for me to stay any longer, *signora*. I've told you everything I know, and I promise to keep in touch by phone. Naturally I'll want to know what has happened to Giovanni, but we've already said our goodbyes.

"A-as for Luke, he has his priesthood duties back in Rome." Maybe if Gaby said the words long enough, she'd start to believe them. "This is not the time for you to be entertaining a houseguest."

"So you know about my eldest son?" she asked too sharply. No doubt Luke's mother had been worried about them spending most of yesterday together.

If she ever found out—

"Y-yes. Giovanni has told me he will be professed in less than a month." Her voice caught.

"That is right." The older woman sounded relieved that Gaby understood the true situation. "He would have taken his final vows much sooner, but my husband's passing made that impossible." There was an uneasy pause. "Luca tells me he spent yesterday helping you trace your family roots."

Heat swamped Gaby's face. "Yes." They were trespassing on shaky ground now. Gaby didn't want to talk or think about Luke anymore. "H-he was able to clear up a mystery about my great-grandmother's true birthplace."

"Yes. He told me," the other woman murmured, eyeing Gaby with a familiar scrutiny that made her uncomfortable.

"I am very grateful to him, *signora*. You must be so proud to have two such remarkable sons." She purposely diverted the direction of the conversation away from Luke.

"I've been very blessed, but as you will understand, I'm devastated to think Giovanni would run away without explanation." Her brown eyes watered. "He's always been the perfect child, so open and obedient."

Gaby knew that wasn't completely true, but she kept silent.

"He and Luca are totally opposites, you know. Luca understands the world and runs his life by his own set of rules. If he went off without a word to me, I'd never question it. He can handle anything because of his brilliance. In time, he will surpass our noble ancestor in greatness and piety."

Gaby had heard of women who were ambitious for their children. But to dream such dreams for Luke seemed almost sacriligious, particularly after what she and Luke had shared in Loretello. The memories still had the power to shake the foundations out from under her.

"Surely the important thing for both your sons is that they be happy." Gaby voiced the opinion beneath her breath.

The older woman nodded. "That is why I am so worried. Something is wrong with my Giovanni who has led a very contented, sheltered life up to now."

"Sheltered or not, he's a remarkably strong individual who prefers to see the goodness of the world," Gaby observed forcefully. "I'm sure there's a rational explanation for what he's done."

"I pray you're right. Poor Efresina loves him so."

Gaby got to her feet, having forgotten all about the other woman Giovanni would never love.

"It's been a privilege to become acquainted with your family. I'm only sorry I can't stay in Urbino longer. The problem is, I've been given a roommate for the tour back to Belgium. If I don't show up, my friend, Joan, will have to be by herself and she doesn't like being alone at night. It would be very unfair to her."

Everything she'd said was true except for the part about her friend hating to be by herself. But Gaby was desperate to get away from Luke. It was hard enough being in his home. But to hear his mother go on about Luke's destiny was only deepening an open wound. She had to get out of there as fast as she could.

"*Signora—*" she implored the older woman who acted as if she still needed convincing to go against Luke's express wishes. "I have no doubts that Luke will eventually find Giovanni. Until then, I can do nothing to ameliorate the situation. I must go."

"Very well," his mother finally conceded. "I will explain to Luke that you are a strong-minded American woman who did not wish to be detained any longer."

Gaby had the idea that deep down, Signora Provere couldn't get rid of her fast enough.

"Thank you. I've been away from my family for a long time and need to get home."

The older woman rang a bell and almost immediately the servant Gaby had seen earlier appeared. "Please bring a car around for Signorina

Holt who must be driven to the university at once. She will need her luggage, as well.''

"*Prego, signora.*''

"*Grazie*, Signora Provere.'' Gaby would have shaken her hand, but Luke's mother surprised her by kissing her on both cheeks instead. Her delight at Gaby's departure was obvious.

"Perhaps it's best that you are returning to the United States. Though you have broken Giovanni's heart, it will mend faster if you are not here. In time I have hopes he will marry Efresina. She's like a daughter to me you know. *Arrivederci, signorina.*''

CHAPTER EIGHT

"WE'RE coming to the border. Pretty soon we're going to go through the St. Gotthard tunnel."

"It's ten miles long, right through the mountains."

Gaby could hear excited conversation all around her and envied the noisy tour group their enthusiasm. Since morning, after barely making it to the university before the bus pulled out of Urbino, she'd tried to put up a brave front around the American friends she hadn't seen for six weeks.

But their arrival in Lake Lugano made her realize they'd be leaving Italy shortly. The pain was as real as if someone had driven a hard fist into her stomach.

"Gaby? What's wrong? You're as white as a sheet."

She avoided Joan's probing stare. "I—I think I ate something that didn't agree with me."

Joan sighed. "It's the atrocious heat. This bus is supposed to be air-conditioned, but I'm still hot."

Gaby hadn't really noticed the temperature. Her heartache was too acute to give thought to her creature comforts. Luke was slipping further and further away from her and there wasn't a thing she could do about it.

"Gina says it's cooler in Switzerland," Joan chatted on. "Tonight we're going to an outdoor yodeling show."

A groan escaped Gaby's throat. After what she'd experienced with Luke, she wondered if she would ever find pleasure in anything again. It was terrifying to think one man could affect your life so completely, that without him there was no joy, no hope.

So far, Gaby hadn't been able to summon the courage to phone Signora Provere. Day after tomorrow, when they reached Brussels, she'd make the call.

Right now she was too afraid to find out what had happened to Giovanni. If he were still missing, then Luke probably hadn't gone back to Rome yet. To phone the palace and hear his voice would destroy her before she'd even begun to deal with her loss.

"Hey, Gina?" someone shouted in the back, drawing Gaby's attention. "How come we're stopping?"

"There's a whole bunch of policemen!" another person cried.

Their vivacious blond Italian tour guide stood up, lighting a cigarette. "I don't know." She exhaled with an Italian flare no foreigner could imitate—another reminder of everything Gaby was about to lose. "Probably they are searching for drugs. It happens. Do not get excited. I will go and find out."

As soon as she got off the bus, speculation intensified. Everyone had a theory about the presence of police who were backing up traffic for miles. Gaby had to admit she was surprised their bus had been stopped. Until now they'd traveled all through Europe without a hitch.

"This is kind of exciting." Joan strained to see what she could because Gaby had the window seat. Together they watched the rapid-fire exchange between Gina and one of the policemen. Her hands were flying.

"Whoa... Gina's upset about something."

Gaby agreed with Joan. Their tour guide, who knew seven languages and could curse along with the best of them, was generally unflappable. But given the tight schedule, a delay would cost them time getting into Lucerne for the evening.

After another five minutes, Gina wheeled around and marched toward the bus, her features set. But instead of getting back on, she shouted something in Italian, and their driver, Mikaele, got off to talk to the police.

"Maybe *he's* in trouble," the girl in front of them theorized.

By now everyone was looking out the right side. To Gaby's astonishment, the police told him to open the panels where the luggage was kept. Mikaele didn't like the delay any more than Gina. He argued volubly, but had no choice except to unload everything.

A group of policemen surrounded him, blocking Gaby's view. Obviously they were checking each tag, searching for something. With thirty-eight students on board, each with two bags, the task was horrendous. Gaby didn't blame him for being upset.

In fact, everyone was complaining. With the motor shut off, there was no air circulating at all.

It seemed like an eternity before Gina climbed on board. The din of noise faded as she started down the aisle followed by two policemen. "Gina's coming this way. She's looking at *you*," Joan whispered in a shaky voice. For no good reason, Gaby felt the hairs stand on the back of her neck.

A cigarette dangled from Gina's full Italian lips as she stopped at their seat. "Gaby, there is no easy way to say this, but you will have to get off the bus and accompany the police to their bureau."

"*What*?"

Gina shrugged her shoulders coolly. "I must admit I am shocked by what the police have discovered in your luggage. Whatever the outcome, you will require help from the American Consulate in Rome. Here is their number. I have written it on my card."

She handed it to Gaby who took it with trembling hands. "I don't understand," she cried.

Gina rolled her eyes. "You look as innocent as the Virgin herself. I, for one, would never have picked you to get into this kind of trouble. For now, I suggest you save any questions or explanations until you retain an advocate."

Panic welled inside her. "But I have to go home!"

"When you have straightened things out, call the main office in London. I will tell them what has happened, and you can proceed from there. The police want your passport."

Gaby couldn't believe this was happening. "It's tucked inside my money belt underneath my clothes," she whispered.

A trace of a smile curved Gina's lips before she turned to the policemen and translated. Both men stared at Gaby with icy contempt. She saw it in their eyes. On top of her crime she was an idiot American, which made her sin a thousand times worse.

"They say you can turn it over to them when they take you to the precinct. It's my opinion that what they found in your luggage was planted by a professional." Gina spoke out of the corner of her mouth, giving her encouragement. "Unfortunately, the burden of proof will rest on you."

Of necessity, Joan had to move so Gaby could get past her. Humiliated and red-faced, Gaby moved out into the aisle.

"If they let you, call me at the hotel in Lucerne tonight and tell me what happened," Joan murmured beneath her breath. "Otherwise, write me."

Gaby pressed her friend's hand before walking down the aisle with the police trailing her footsteps.

"Good luck, Gaby," both Gina and Mikaele called to her as she got off the bus.

An hour later, Gaby found herself at police headquarters in Lugano. She surrendered her passport and was booked and finger-printed. No one would tell her details about her arrest. She could make no phone calls. They informed her that the consulate in Rome would not be available until the next morning.

That's when she broke down and begged them to call the palace in Urbino, convinced that one word in her defense from the House of Provere would do more to exonerate her than all the red tape the American Consulate could accomplish.

But the police ignored her entreaty. To her horror, Gaby realized she would have to spend the night on a cot in a jail cell like a common criminal.

Only the knowledge that she knew she was innocent of any wrongdoing kept her from losing her sanity. That and the fact that as soon as she could do anything at all about her situation, she'd phone Signora Provere. Surely Luke was back home by now. With his power and influence, she'd be freed in an instant.

How ironic that this morning she couldn't get away from him fast enough. He'd ordered her to stay with his mother until his return. If she'd done his bidding, she wouldn't be locked up with no hope of being freed before morning.

A shudder racked her body. All the ifs in the world wouldn't change what had happened. She had run away from him, and tonight she was paying the price.

Dear God—what she'd give to see him standing outside the bars of her cell!

Defeated for the moment by her situation, she lay facedown on the cot in the dark, burying her face in the crook of her arm. Unfortunately other thoughts, all negative, began to creep into her psyche, paralyzing her with new fear.

It was possible Luke might not be available right away. If he were still looking for Giovanni, it could be several days before he even knew about her situation, let alone had the time to do something about it.

The more she considered what Signora Provere's reaction might be, the more she worried that Luke's mother wouldn't be willing to help her. She wanted Gaby out of Giovanni's life and wasn't the least bit happy that Luke had spent any time with her.

To make matters worse, Gaby was from Las Vegas, a place for the riffraff of American society in the older woman's mind. No doubt she would consider it more than a possibility that Gaby had stolen something not belonging to her. She would endorse any punishment the Italian authorities chose to mete out to her.

Exhausted from her ordeal, overwhelmed by all the emotions buffeting her body, she closed her eyes and gave in to the temptation to think forbidden thoughts about Luke.

"*Signorina*? Holt?"

Gaby thought she heard her name called and lifted her head, groggy because she must have fallen asleep for a while. A faint light at the end of the hall outlined two masculine silhouettes.

"Yes?" she answered tentatively and sat up, aware there were marks on her cheek where she'd been lying on her braid. One of the policemen unlocked her cell to allow the other man inside, then locked it again and walked away.

Gaby scrambled to her feet, suddenly frightened. "W-who are you?"

"Shh, Gaby. Talk softly so no one can hear you but me."

She blinked in the darkness. The voice sounded so familiar, but it couldn't be, could it? "*Giovanni*?" she whispered in shock.

"Yes. Sit down, Gaby, before you faint."

She half fell against the cot. "What are you doing here when you're supposed to be recovering from your accident? What's going on? Why have I been arrested? Please tell me. Why did you disappear? Your family is frantic."

"Be patient and I will answer all your questions. But we don't have much time. I must be gone from here before Luca comes."

Luke was coming? Her heart began to pound outrageously. "All right. I'm listening."

She couldn't imagine what Giovanni was about and wondered if she was in the middle of a strange dream.

"First, I have to ask you a question and you must answer it with total honesty because God is listening."

This was Giovanni talking to her, but he was being so mysterious. More than that, he sounded different, older, so solemn . . .

"W-what is the question?"

"You were with my brother all day yesterday, isn't that true?"

Gaby moaned in turmoil. This was the hardest thing she'd ever had to admit to in her life because she would never have hurt Giovanni intentionally. "Yes," she said with tears in her voice.

"Tell me everything that happened from the moment you saw him until you parted company last night."

Obviously this was of vital concern to Giovanni or he wouldn't be vetting her like this in a jail cell. Perhaps Luke was in some kind of trouble with church authorities because of her. Gaby was beside herself with anxiety.

"He caught up with me in Assisi," she began breathlessly. "He said that he'd p-promised you to escort me to the ball, and intended to take me back to Urbino so Luciana could do my hair."

"That's very interesting, considering the fact that my brother informed me he could not carry out my wishes and had to be back in Rome without fail," Giovanni murmured as if to himself. "Go on."

By now Gaby was shaking, consumed by guilt. Giovanni was a very intuitive person. *He knew the truth about her and Luke.* But for some reason she didn't understand, he wouldn't let it go until he'd wrung every detail from her. This was a nightmare in a new dimension.

"I took the early bus out of town because I wanted to visit Assisi before I left Italy. H-he found me up on the ramparts of the castle and insisted that I return to the palace with him."

"Which means he followed you there," Giovanni muttered.

Gaby hid her face in her hands. "Yes."

"Did you spend the whole day in Assisi?"

A little sob escaped her throat. "No— We— We drove to an inn for lunch." Every revelation damned them a little more in Giovanni's eyes.

"Tell me about it," he persisted in a calm voice.

"Why do you want to hear all this, Giovanni?" she cried, knowing this had to be bringing him excruciating pain.

"Just humor me, please. Is that such a difficult thing to do for a brother? You told my mother that you loved me like one."

"I do!" She moaned the words once more. Hot tears trickled down her cheeks. *He'd already been in touch with Signora Provere.*

In the next breath Gaby told him everything she could remember about their meal. "Afterward, we drove to Loretello, but he stopped at Arcevia first."

"Ah—to find your great-grandmother's farm."

"Yes."

There was a slight pause. "And did you find it, Gaby?"

She nodded, but no sound would come out.

"Something happened while you were there."

"Yes." She moistened her lips anxiously. "Through the parish records, L-Luke found out that my relative was probably born somewhere in or near Rome. She was brought to Loretello to be raised by the Ridolfi family and remained there until she ran off with her future husband."

"That is all very fascinating. But I'm talking about you and my brother." The ghastly silence almost destroyed her. "Did he kiss you?"

A groan came out of Gaby. She couldn't stop the convulsions of her body.

"All you have to do is tell me yes or no."

She sucked in her breath. "Yes." The blood was pounding in her ears.

"The way a man kisses a woman when he desires her?"

Gaby jumped off the cot, holding her arms to her chest. "Yes."

"Gaby—" he whispered in a shaken voice. "Did you kiss him back the same way? It's the last question I'll ask of you."

She wanted to die. "Yes."

He crossed himself.

"Oh, Giovanni." She broke down weeping. "Please forgive me. Forgive us. It just happened. Luke is as tormented as I am. I swear we never meant to hurt you."

"You haven't hurt me," he murmured in a strange tone of voice. "Thank you for telling me the truth. You've heard the wise-old adage that the truth shall make you free."

"Yes, but I also know that deep down it has shocked you and caused you pain, whatever you say to the contrary. What are you going to do now?" she cried in real concern for his welfare.

Instead of answering her, he leaned forward and kissed her forehead. "It won't be long before Luca effects your release. As a last favor to me, please don't tell him I was here and forced a confession from you. It would hurt him too much. He has always tried to protect me. Leave him that illusion, I beg of you, dearest Gaby."

His earnestness confounded her. "I promise," she vowed in a choked voice, wiping her eyes. "But what if the guards tell him you were here?"

"They won't," was all he would say on the subject.

"Does he know you're all right?"

"I'm sure mother has told him. I know I can count on you to keep your word. Enjoy your trip home, Gaby."

"Wait—" she called as he turned and tapped on the bars of the cell. "I want to know where you're going, what you're going to do. Don't shut me out!"

"There's no time," came the cryptic reply before the guard reappeared to open the gate. She clung to the bars long after Giovanni had gone, pressing her head against the metal in despair.

His niceness was terrifying because she knew it hid scalding pain. She would have done anything to prevent him from learning the truth. Now that he'd heard the words from her own lips, she would never be able to forgive herself.

But she'd made a promise not to tell Luke about his brother's visit. It was a promise she intended to keep for Giovanni's sake. There could be no point in wounding Luke who would always carry the pain of their betrayal of Giovanni in his heart.

At least he could return to Rome believing that his brother knew nothing about their romantic interlude. All three of them would go on to pursue their separate lives. It was the way it had to be.

She went over everything in her mind, trying to put the pieces together. Whatever the reason for her arrest, the Provere family had known about it in time for Giovanni to come all the way to Lugano.

But he was leaving it to Luke to help her out of the mess she'd unwittingly gotten herself into. Now that he assumed they were lovers, Giovanni was too much of a gentleman to ever interfere.

Just the thought of Luke coming to the jail sent her heart tripping out of control. She felt like jumping out of her skin, but there was no place to go. After pacing back and forth waiting for the first sight of him, she finally gave up the vigil and flung herself on the cot.

It was probably close to midnight. Something had to be holding him up. Maybe he'd decided to wait until morning to do anything about her situation.

Heaving a forlorn sigh that resounded in the cell, she turned toward the wall, confused and broken. It was when her limbs started to grow heavy that the overhead light went on.

She heard her name cried out, followed by a burst of Italian invective delivered in a deep voice that sounded so fierce it couldn't possibly belong to anyone but Luke.

Gaby rolled over on her back in time to see the intimidated guard who had trouble undoing the lock. Then Luke came striding toward her like an avenging prince, his handsome features darkened by lines of fury.

"*Per Dio!*" he raged. In his anger he was truly magnificent. She caught a few words like barbaric and criminal, and there was something said about it not being the fourteenth century. Then he got down on his haunches and cupped her face in his hands.

"Are you all right, Gabriella?" His glittering black gaze seemed to devour her. She watched his sensual mouth twist into a white line of anger.

"Have they given you anything to eat or drink?"
All the while he was emoting, she could feel his
thumbs following the delicate mold of her cheeks.

Gaby was so happy to see him, she couldn't talk
or think. All she could do was shake her head.
Another shocking epithet escaped his lips. It
produced a guard who immediately brought her a
glass of cold water.

Once Luke helped her to sit up, she needed no
urging to drink thirstily. "Oh, that tasted good,"
she murmured after draining the contents.

A nerve throbbed along his jaw. "Have they allowed you to use the restroom?"

"No."

"*Mio Dio*!" he thundered once more. "No
matter what they think you've done, they had no
right to treat you in this despicable manner." His
eyes narrowed. "Before I'm through, someone's
going to pay heavily for this."

"I—I've heard about foreign jails. Maybe ours
at home are just as bad. This is my first experience."

His chest heaved. "When I couldn't find
Giovanni, I arrived home to discover many shocks.
You'd not only disobeyed my instructions about
leaving, but the police had contacted Mother to let
them know you were in custody. You were falsely
arrested, but I've straightened it out."

Relieved, Gaby admitted, "I begged them to call
you."

"Considering the way you've been treated, it's a
miracle they followed through to reach me."

"The police wouldn't tell me anything, but my
tour guide, Gina, said something valuable was

found in my luggage. She suspected it was planted there.''

Gaby heard his sharp intake of breath. ''Your guide was right.'' He was obviously trying to control himself and didn't realize his own strength. The hand on her shoulder tightened almost painfully, but heaven forgive her, she craved his touch, the warmth of his strong chest where her head rested. She'd stay in this condition forever if it meant being this close to him.

''Gina told me to call the American Consulate in Rome, but the police sergeant said they couldn't be reached until tomorrow.''

Perhaps he wasn't aware that one of his hands slid up and down her braid, bringing every cell in her body alive. ''They lied to you,'' he muttered in contempt. ''There is an emergency number for someone in your circumstances. But no matter now. If you're ready, we'll go to the office and gather up your things.''

Basking in Luke's strength and protection, Gaby had no desire to move. If she could spend the night on this cot with him, it would be all she ever asked of life. But of course that wasn't possible.

Because of the precariousness of her situation, they'd both let down their guard. She had to remember that if it hadn't been for the arrest, they would never have seen each other again. The thought produced a low moan he must have heard because he continued to steady her once she was on her feet.

''If you need food, I'll send one of the guards for something to eat.''

"No, no. I'm fine. Honestly. I—it's just that I was asleep when you came in and I'm still trying to wake up."

His jaw hardened. "This airless room isn't healthy. Come." With his hand at the back of her waist, he ushered her out of the cell and down the hall to the main office where the balding police sergeant sat at his desk.

At Luke's approach, he stood up, his manner totally deferential. Luke fired several questions in Italian. A volley of comments followed. Then the other man undid a safe and handed him a large manila envelope which Gaby assumed contained the stolen item.

Luke didn't bother to unseal it. Instead, he escorted her to another room where she saw her two suitcases sitting on the floor. The contents were dumped on top of a rectangular wooden table. Other than three chairs, the room was as bare as the jail cell. The sergeant excused himself and shut the door.

Gaby was upset about the cavalier handling of her things, but she was more curious about the stolen property. Her eyes appealed to Luke. "A-aren't you going to open it?"

His dark gaze searched hers for endless moments. "I don't need to. The sergeant told me the tip-off about the jewelry came from the palace."

Gaby's brows formed a slight frown. "What jewelry?"

"The headdress Giovanni wanted you to wear to the ball."

Her rounded chin shot up. "Something worth almost a million dollars was in *my* luggage?"

"Let's take a look, shall we?"

With one fluid motion, he undid the top and pulled the pearl hair ornament out of the envelope.

A noise escaped her throat. "The last time I saw it, we were at the hospital visiting Giovanni. How on earth could it have gotten in my suitcase?"

A shadow crossed over Luke's face. "As your tour guide said, someone planted it to make it look as if you'd stolen it."

"But Giovanni was the last one to have it."

"No, *I* was," Luke corrected her. "After visiting Giovanni the next morning, I took it home with me and gave it to Luciana for safekeeping."

Silence stretched between them. Gaby was trying to figure it out. "You said Luciana adores Giovanni. Do you think she was angry with me because I stayed away instead of going to the ball as Giovanni wanted?"

"Angry enough to want to get you into this kind of trouble?" Luke questioned darkly. "I don't think so. Luciana has been with the family for years. For her to risk imprisonment makes absolutely no sense."

Gaby's head lowered. "It seems that someone in your household hated me enough to get me arrested—someone who knew where to find the jewelry and had access to my luggage this morning."

Luke's features looked chiseled. "Efresina doesn't live at the palace."

"Your m-mother does..." she said in a quiet voice.

His chest rose and fell harshly. "No, Gabriella. She was very unkind to you at dinner, but she would never do anything to risk losing the love of her sons."

"Luke, I'm sorry I said anything about your mother. Actually, she apologized to me this morning."

"That's good," he almost growled. "She should have done it before you left the palace the night of the dinner."

Gaby rubbed her palms over her hips in an unconscious gesture of frustration, but Luke watched the movement with such intensity, she trembled.

"W-what about the servant who brought my bags in from the car?"

"Giuseppi?" Just the way he said the man's name told Gaby that Luke cared deeply for him. In an aside he murmured, "He's been with us longer than Luciana."

She folded her arms. "Then that leaves Giovanni, only he wasn't there."

"*Wasn't he*?" Luke rasped with an abruptness that caught her off guard.

She couldn't look at him right then, not when she knew that Giovanni had been in Lugano, that he'd sworn her to secrecy.

"A network of people were out looking for Giovanni all day," Luke muttered blackly, rubbing the back of his neck absently. "But it was as if he'd disappeared off the face of the earth."

At his words, a shiver chased across her skin. "Luke, I just remembered something he once told me." What she had to say wouldn't be disloyal to Giovanni.

"He said that during the Renaissance, secret rooms and passages were built in the palace for the family's protection. Because I thought he was a palace employee, I assumed that was part of the knowledge he had learned to inform the public."

"*Mio Dio*!" Luke cried, comprehension illuminating his puzzled countenance. "Why didn't I think of that sooner? Gabriella—you've just supplied me with the key to a very complicated riddle."

"What are you saying?"

He began pacing. "On the surface, Giovanni has always appeared very sweet and straightforward. But something has changed him out of all recognition. While I've been away, his behavior has undergone a drastic transformation. Like one of our more notorious Provere ancestors, Giovanni has become a cunning master of mind games and intrigue."

She shook her head. "I don't understand."

He sucked in his breath, straightening to his full height. "It began with the phone call to Rome." His voice grated. "With each convoluted step, he has managed to throw our lives into utter chaos."

A hand went to her throat. "You think he put the jewelry in my luggage?"

"I know he did, then he alerted the police. It's all part of a plan."

Deep down, Gaby believed that, too. There could be no other explanation for Giovanni's appearance at the jail, his ability to come and go as he pleased. It had to prove he'd been behind her incarceration. Right now she wished she hadn't made him any promises.

"You're right, Luke." Her voice shook. "He's been playing games from the moment I first met him at the museum."

Luke grimaced. "They're about to end. He's not a little boy anymore. As soon as I get you out of here, we're going back to Urbino. We'll find him in one of those labyrinths beneath the palace and we'll confront him together."

Much as she wanted to go with him, be with him as long as he wanted her, she knew it was impossible. Now was the time to be strong and back away from him, both mentally as well as physically.

"No, Luke. You two brothers need to solve this problem without an audience. I've said my goodbyes to Giovanni. My family is expecting me home." Her voice sounded ragged because she couldn't deal with the pain. "I have to go."

CHAPTER NINE

LUKE'S face looked wiped of expression, but the fact that he didn't argue with her felt like a second death.

He stood next to the table, a tall, rigid, powerful figure in black. She saw his gaze dart to her underwear, then a pair of canvas shoes, a Levi's skirt and three cotton tops like the pink one she was wearing, hose, drip-dry shorty pajamas, one pair of white shorts, and a dilapidated, one-piece faded black bathing suit.

Her toiletries and blow-dryer lay askew amid the absurd, cheap trinkets she'd picked up at various tourist traps since her arrival in Europe in June.

Because she was on a tight budget, she hadn't been able to buy anything expensive, but she refused to go home to her family and friends empty-handed. She had opted to buy a whole bunch of fun, joky gifts.

By the quirk of one raven-winged eyebrow, she could tell that the illustrious Luke Provere was unaccustomed to mingling with a common student and tourist like herself. He was probably appalled at the cluttered scene before him.

To her surprise he started poking around, as if to satisfy his curiosity. Unwillingly drawn by the play of muscles across his shoulders and back, she watched him pick up one item, then another for examination.

He held up a miniature iron maiden torture device and a trace of a smile broke the corner of his mouth. "For someone with such an angelic face as yours, no one would guess at the Machiavellian mind lurking inside."

She smiled in spite of her pain. "My brother, Ted, plays Dungeons & Dragons. When he finds out what it was used for, he'll love it," she defended.

"No doubt," he muttered. "And this?" From his fingers dangled a leather strap with a Swiss cow bell on the end.

"That's for my brother, Wayne, who works on a ranch."

"It's too small for a cow."

Her smile broadened. "I was thinking of his dog, Grafton."

"Grafton?" His incredulity was more marked because of his accent. In other circumstances, she would have laughed.

Next, he pulled out a collapsible leaning Tower of Pisa. By depressing a button, it fell to one side.

"That's for my father. He's a fiddler."

Luke cast her a hooded glance over his shoulder. "He plays the violin?"

"Not exactly. He's the nervous type. Always touching things, pacing the floor. The tower will keep him busy."

"With a daughter like you, I'm beginning to understand."

Ignoring the blush that tinted her cheeks he pulled out an assortment of manufactured feudal weapons including a mace, a ball and chain, and crossbow purchased in Carcassonne. Another eyebrow quirked.

"My little brother Robbie loves knights and castles," she proclaimed before he could say anything.

Finally he came to an Eiffel Tower which she explained would serve as an outdoor thermometer for Scott's Jeep, and a pair of Egyptian *obélisque* earrings for her mom which she'd bought in Paris.

"Those snake rings from Morocco are for my friends," she commented when he'd come to the end of her treasures, fingering each one carefully.

After reflection, "No presents for yourself?"

"Except the ones I steal?" she joked, but it failed miserably. His hands had formed into fists. Her heartache intensified because Giovanni's spectre loomed too heavily over their lives. "A-actually I shipped my Italian texts and a few picture books home several days ago."

Evidently unable to help himself, Luke reached for one more paper-enveloped package which the police had left half opened.

Gaby had forgotten about that souvenir and moved quickly to intercept him, but it was too late. In a lightning gesture he'd already pulled out the simple inexpensive, eight-inch statuette of Jesus purchased in the Vatican city.

"Out of all the souvenirs you could have chosen to take home for a memory, you purchased *this* for yourself?" He sounded stunned.

"Yes," she defended. "I had to earn all my own money to come to Europe. As you can see, I've lived at the poverty level for some time now. I only had a hundred dollars to buy all my souvenirs."

His face closed up. "Once again you've misunderstood me. I wasn't referring to its monetary value."

Her face grew warm. Suitably chastened she said, "I'm sorry. I-it's just that we come from such vastly different backgrounds, even I can see how this must seem to you." Her voice wobbled.

"But even if it is cheap, the beautiful face on that little figure resembles my idea of what Jesus really looked like. I—I bought it when I first went to Rome and plan to keep it on my dresser at home."

They both stared at the graphic reminder of the tremendous gulf which was about to separate Luke from the rest of the world.

Damn. She could feel tears starting and tore her eyes away first. Quickly, before she lost it, she started packing her suitcases.

Luke put the souvenir back in the paper and handed it to her. "Are you an active churchgoer, Gabriella?" came the low-pitched question.

She shouldn't have been surprised by his query, not when Luke was the one doing the asking. It was just that they'd never discussed religion, or their views on theology.

"Yes," she murmured quietly, closing the last zipper. "I can't imagine what my life would be like without my faith to cling to."

With her packing done, she picked up both cases. "If you would be kind enough to help me get a taxi to the train station, I'll take the next one to Brussels and sleep on the way. My plane doesn't leave until the day after tomorrow so I'll arrive there with time to spare."

"You shouldn't be in a train station alone this late at night." That tone of command came so naturally to him, he probably wasn't aware of it. But Gaby knew it was unwise to be in his company any longer. It took all her strength of will not to beg him to take her someplace private and make love to her.

To arm herself against his irresistible charisma she retorted, "That's nonsense. I've been doing everything on my own for a long time and can take care of myself."

"A few karate moves no matter how well taught to you by your brothers won't protect you from a pack of men intent on only one thing. You're coming with me."

"No, Luke!" His declaration terrified her and she backed away from him. But her reaction only seemed to arouse his ire. In one swift movement, his hand snaked out to grasp her wrist, making escape impossible.

Submitting her to a withering glance, he said, "Until you leave my country, you will remain under my protection whether you accompany me willingly or not." His hold tightened.

"But you need to get back to the palace and find Giovanni," she cried, frantically trying to think of reasons to get away from him. "Your mother must be terribly upset with you gone."

"She'll live." With the envelope under one arm, he took the heaviest suitcase from her and started pulling her toward the door. Gaby had to run to keep up with him.

"W-where are we going?"

"To a hotel where we will get something to eat and a good night's sleep. First thing in the morning I'll put you on a plane to Brussels."

The thought of being alone with him any place private set her heart racing out of rhythm. "Luke, you don't understand. I can't affor—"

"*Basta*! There are times when you drive me too far, Gabriella." Another savage oath silenced her. "My brother's machinations have put you in this situation. It goes without saying that I will make restitution for what he's done."

Before she knew it, they'd exited the police station and he deposited her and the luggage in a rental car. When Luke had heard she was in jail, he must have taken a plane to Lugano. Fresh guilt kept her silent as he drove through the quiet streets. She was afraid to say a word in case she unleashed another violent reaction in him.

Purposely keeping her head turned so she couldn't look at him, she noticed they were leaving the city proper. Before long they reached a road bordering the shimmering water. Every so often she glimpsed a fabulous villa through the foliage. This was a residential area. Only the very wealthy could afford to live along this section of the sophisticated lakeside resort.

"There aren't any hotels here," she blurted in trepidation, forgetting her vow not to talk.

"That's true."

"You lied to me!"

"Yes," he admitted with infuriating relish. "If I'd told you I was taking you to a property my family owns and uses on occasion, you would have refused to come and forced me to carry you bodily from the jail. It was better this way, don't you agree?" he questioned in a silky tone.

"How can you even ask me that?" Her whole body surged with exploding emotion. After their experience in Loretello, she didn't trust herself to go anywhere with him.

"I'm well known in my country, Gabriella." His deep voice grated. "I didn't tell you that to impress you. Only to remind you that for obvious reasons, I prefer to avoid scandal. If someone saw me taking a woman who looks like you to a hotel in the middle of the night, the paparazzi would get wind of it and your reputation would suffer along with mine."

He was right. It *would* look terrible. Luke couldn't afford that kind of talk this close to taking his vows.

She bowed her head, unable to argue with his logic. It was amazing that no matter the issue, he always found a way to reduce her concerns to so much trivia.

"I phoned the housekeeper from the jail and instructed her to prepare a light meal. It won't be the Trattoria Alberto, but we won't starve."

He shouldn't have reminded her of that halcyon day. The memories were too haunting and raw. "Thank you for being so thoughtful," she murmured in a subdued tone.

"It's the least I can do after the ordeal you've been put through today."

"I don't imagine this has been easy for you, either," she conceded. After a slight pause, "Did you have to get special permission to be away from Rome this long?"

She felt his body tauten. "Would it shock you if I told you I left without permission?"

Gaby shuddered involuntarily.

"I can see that I have," he observed dryly.

Fear for him made perspiration break out on her brow. "Are you in serious trouble then?"

"Yes. Nothing should take precedence over God."

Anger warred with anxiety. "Giovanni knew better than to phone you and place demands which could jeopardize your work."

Luke made a left turn onto a private road and they started a climb through the flowering shrubs. "My brother may have described you as a paragon without equal, but rest assured the decision to come home was entirely mine," he drawled. "If you must be upset, then blame my unorthodox curiosity which overcame duty."

Aghast, she cried, "What will you do?"

"I'll face the consequences as soon as I take care of unfinished business."

"You mean Giovanni." Her voice shook.

"*Sì, signorina.*"

Gaby had been so caught up in what he'd told her, she hadn't realized he'd stopped in front of a Ticino-styled villa with a deck on the upper story. The lights inside beckoned.

She looked behind her shoulder. "I'll need—"

"I'll bring them both," he cut in mildly, reminding her that he'd seen *everything* she owned and had watched her pack up her things without taking care what went where.

Prickly warmth sent her scurrying from the car, only to come to a complete standstill when she saw a sixtyish-looking Italian woman just inside the open door of the chalet-type domicile.

She greeted Luke like visiting royalty, her raisin eyes misting as she crossed herself and curtsied in front of him, kissing his hand.

A sharp stab of pain made Gaby turn away. The woman's touching homage to the man she saw as a priest came as a tremendous shock to Gaby.

Giovanni's words flooded back, haunting her. Luke had been training for the religious role all his life. Her instantaneous adoration reflected that humbling truth.

Gaby had no business here, no business at all.

"Signorina Holt, this is Bianca," he said in the bland voice of the perfect host. "She speaks English very well. We'll follow her to the room she has prepared for you."

The plump housekeeper gave Gaby an incurious glance before she led them across tile floors and up the stairs to a charming bedroom facing the lake.

While Luke deposited her bags on the floor, Gaby stared at the quaint simplicity of the cozy villa which came as a surprise after the sumptuousness of the palace. Instead of gilt, statuary and tapestries, there was a comfortable-looking four-poster bed with hand-carved wooden furnishings. French doors opened out onto the veranda.

"I hope you'll be comfortable here. When you've refreshed yourself, come downstairs to the kitchen."

Gaby swung back around, not meeting his eyes. "I-if you don't mind, I'm not feeling very well and would like to go directly to bed."

Having said those words she got the distinct impression that she'd angered him. A ruddy flush dulled his cheeks. But she didn't have a choice. If they'd been alone, he would have argued with her until he'd broken her down and forced her to eat a meal with him.

Under no circumstances could she allow that to happen. At Loretello, Gaby's unwise behavior had tempted Luke to show his human side. Tonight she was weakening where her own strength of will was concerned. All it would take was one smoldering glance from him and she'd lose the little self-control she had left.

Like a godsend, Bianca's presence acted as the perfect buffer. Gaby would cling to the housekeeper in order to distance herself from Luke until she could leave Italy altogether.

Ignoring his well-honed physique still poised near the doorway, she addressed the older woman. "I have a headache, *signora*. Do you keep any medicine here?"

"*Sì, signorina.*"

"Would you show me please?" she asked before Luke could offer his assistance.

The older woman nodded, indicating Gaby should follow her into the ensuite bathroom, the one place Luke couldn't accompany them.

Clearly not pleased, he watched her enter the spotless interior and disappear from his narrowed line of vision. To her relief, Bianca shut the door and pulled a bottle of pills from the cabinet.

Gaby turned on the shower taps so they couldn't be overheard. "Thank you, Bianca. If you'd be kind enough to bring my bags in here, I'll wash and get ready for bed."

"I'll bring up a tray in case you get hungry later."

"That's very thoughtful of you, but it's Father Luca who needs your help." In a confiding tone Gaby whispered, "I am a close friend of his brother Giovanni who was in a car accident."

The older woman looked shocked and crossed herself. "Is he all right?"

"He will be, but the poor Father has been worried about him and hasn't slept for several nights. Please do everything you can to make him comfortable. Force him to eat something. If you have a little *Verdicchio* wine, that might relax him. Then let him sleep in tomorrow morning. He must be well rested before he returns to Rome."

"Of course." The housekeeper nodded, obviously thrilled to be given such an important task. No doubt she loved fussing over the man she revered so much. "You can depend on me."

"I knew it." She pressed the other woman's hand, praying she'd won her confidence. "One more thing—'' she murmured, eyeing the phone by the bed. ''I'll be leaving before he awakens. Say nothing about that to him or he will insist on driving me to the airport. You know how good and kind he is. How he loves to take care of everyone else.''

The woman's eyes brimmed over. ''He is a saint.''

A sad smile broke out on Gaby's face. ''He's the most wonderful man I've ever known. But this is one time when we all need to watch over him. You understand what I'm saying?''

''*Sì, signorina.* I will do everything I can for him.''

''God bless you, Bianca.''

''And you, *signorina*.'' She crossed herself again.

Before the housekeeper left the bathroom, Gaby asked for the address of the villa so she could tell the taxi exactly where to come in the morning.

When she heard the door click, Gaby crossed her fingers and stepped beneath the spray. Since coming to Italy, she'd learned to conserve water by getting in and out of the shower as fast as possible. But because of her precarious circumstances, she remained inside for a long time and washed her hair. Anything to drag out the moment. Hopefully by the time she climbed into bed, Luke would have eaten and gone to his room for the night.

Finally, when she'd dried her hair enough to braid it, she crept into the bedroom, shut off the light and dove beneath the covers.

No sooner had she turned on her side than there was a tap on the door. It had to be Luke. Bianca would have walked in without permission. Gaby started to shake and couldn't stop.

"Gabriella?"

Though he only whispered her name, she could feel the deep intonation pierce her skin to the innermost core of her.

More than anything in the world she wanted to answer him. Instead, she got on her knees under the covers and prayed with all her might that he would go away.

He called her name again.

Gaby writhed in pain. If she encouraged him to come into the room, there was no telling what might happen. She couldn't live with that on her conscience and continued to beg for strength to resist him.

After a while, she had reason to believe he'd gone away. Her prayers were answered. For the rest of the night she sat propped up in bed with tears streaming down her face, watching the lights twinkle around the shoreline of the lake.

At dawn, she quietly slid from the bed and got dressed, then phoned the operator to get the number of the taxi station. Within a few minutes, she'd called for her ride.

With that accomplished, she went out on the veranda where the spectacular view of Lake Lugano spread before her like a fairyland. But right now her main concern was escape.

There were steps leading up one side of the villa. If she climbed over the railing, it was just a small jump to freedom.

She went back inside for her suitcases, then lowered them noiselessly over the railing into the garden, one at a time. After shutting the sliding door, she went back out on the veranda and heaved herself down to the stairs.

Once her bags were in hand, she crept through the underbrush to the road where she hid beneath a flowering tree. Luke would never be able to see her from the villa windows.

The longest ten minutes of her life went by while she stood there terrified because Luke might discover her disappearance and come running outside to see where she'd gone.

But providence was with her, because she finally saw a taxi turn up the lane. Without waiting another moment, she ran toward it, hoping the driver wouldn't come abreast of the villa.

"Drive me to the train station, *per favore*," she cried in her best Italian, jumping in the back seat with her suitcases. "*Sono in ritardo*." She had told him she was late so that he'd hurry.

The middle-aged driver turned around and grinned with typical male appreciation. "*Capisco, signorina*."

All Italian cabdrivers were insane so it didn't take him long to reach their destination. Luckily the morning traffic had been light. There were fewer near-mishaps than usual.

She got out of the car dragging her suitcases, threw some lire at him and started running. It didn't matter which train was in the station. She'd take whichever one would get her out of town the fastest, even if it was going the wrong way. She could always get off at the next main station and regroup.

As fate would have it, a local commuter was heading south to Milan. Without blinking an eye she bought a one-way ticket and promptly dashed outside, looking for the right track. The train was just starting to pull out of the station.

She ran alongside it and literally tossed her suitcases into the passageway, then jumped on board. Out of breath, she stood on trembling limbs, clinging to the handrails on either side of the steps.

In the throes of agony, she felt her life pass before her as Lugano eventually disappeared from view and Luca Provere with it.

CHAPTER TEN

"GABY?"

At the sound of Wayne's voice, she paused in the act of washing the plates from lunch and looked over her shoulder at her brother who was putting on his heavy-duty gloves.

"I'm going out on the south range with Will for a couple of hours to do some fencing. When I get back, we'll take that ride up the saddle and camp out."

"Don't hurry on my account. I'm not in the mood to go anywhere, but thanks just the same."

He shoved a weathered cowboy hat on his blond head. "You know something, little sister? You haven't been in the mood since you got home from Italy. It's past time you told me about the man who has put you into such a severe depression."

"I'm not in a severe depression!" she snapped with uncharacteristic sharpness. White-faced, she resumed her task at the sink of the trailer home provided for his use as foreman of the Red Fork Ranch.

He chewed on a piece of straw, eyeing her shrewdly. "No? Dropping ten pounds, and not going to the university when you're two quarters away from graduating, is what I call pretty damn depressing. If that weren't enough, you're living up here with no salary to speak of, no girlfriends, and no hope in hell of finding an eligible male. All in all, you've changed so drastically, I'm beginning to think the folks are right.''

She blinked in alarm. ''What do you mean?''

''They want you to get professional help. I agree with them.''

''I don't need counselling.''

''Then you're going to have to prove it and talk to me when I get back later. Otherwise, I'm booting you out of here for your own good.''

''No, Wayne! Please!'' she cried in panic at her brother's defection. But he'd gone out the door and there was no calling him back. Once he dug in his heels, that was it.

Since her return, he'd given her her space, had made no demands. Wayne had always been her idol. She'd always been able to count on him. Or so she'd thought...

Gaby clung to the edge of the counter. The fact that Wayne agreed with her parents about her needing help disturbed her greatly because deep inside she was beginning to believe it herself.

Since her flight from Europe, each day had passed like a hundred years. There was a bleakness to her existence which had started to frighten her. Instead of time being the great healer, the opposite seemed to have occurred. Today was October fifth. Luke had been professed for a week now. Why couldn't she forget him? What was wrong with her?

In an effort to numb herself to the scalding pain of bittersweet memories, she finished the dishes and attacked her housekeeping chores with a vengeance.

By the time an hour had passed and there was nothing else to clean, she came to the conclusion that she'd better unload to her brother before she had a complete breakdown.

With hot tears gushing from her eyes, she flung herself facedown on the couch, wishing she could go to sleep and never wake up. Crying spells had become a habit she couldn't seem to break.

She knew she was pathetic and should pull herself together before Wayne got back. But drugged by her own inertia, she stayed curled up until she heard the sound of a motor.

Since there was no more dirt road beyond the trailer, most likely one of the hands was coming up to talk to Wayne about a problem. Then again, someone could be lost.

Mortified to be caught this way, Gaby jumped to her bare feet. But she didn't have time to check the mirror before she heard footsteps outside followed by a rap on the trailer door. No way could she open it in her condition.

"If you're looking for Wayne, he's gone to the south range and won't be back until supper." She'd been sobbing so hard, her voice sounded like a foghorn.

"I'm not looking for Wayne," came a low, masculine voice, distinctly unwestern.

Puzzled, she took a peek out the curtained window and saw an unfamiliar Buick Skylark parked next to Wayne's truck. Everyone who worked on the ranch drove pickups, which meant the man outside was a stranger.

For no good reason, a frisson of apprehension made her stiffen. Wayne had always warned her about keeping the trailer locked when he was gone. Thank heaven he'd locked it on his way out.

Struggling to sound calm, she said, "You must want Mr. Hayes, the owner of the Red Fork. If you'll go back down the road a half mile and turn left, you'll come to his ranch house." At this point she wasn't about to admit that Will wasn't home, either.

"I haven't flown ten thousand miles to see the owner. *Per Dio*, Gabriella. Open the door before I break it in."

Her heart gave a great thump.

It couldn't be... It just couldn't be!

When she'd first heard Luke's voice behind her on the castle ramparts in Assisi, she'd thought she was hallucinating.

But hearing that same voice on a hidden ranch in the Sierra Nevada mountains of North America meant she had really lost her mind. Slowly, Gaby backed away from the door.

"If there's someone inside with you, get rid of him. *Now*!"

She stood there paralyzed with shock, unable to make as much as a squeaking sound. Seconds later she heard the crack of splintering wood and suddenly Luke appeared inside the trailer, dwarfing it with his dark, powerful frame.

Her blue eyes widened in total disbelief to see the true Duke of Urbino standing in all his magnificence not two feet away from her. It didn't matter that he was dressed in Western jeans and a crewneck navy pullover. Nothing could disguise his striking aura, his sophistication.

Lines marred his unforgettable male features. With undisguised intimacy, his devouring black gaze traveled over her face and figure.

She was wearing one of Wayne's Western shirts with the sleeves pushed up above her elbows. The hem hung lower than her cutoffs. It probably looked like she'd thrown it on in haste, and didn't have a stitch on underneath. With no lipstick, and her hair loose and disheveled, she could imagine what he might be thinking.

Judging by the way his hands worked into fists at his side, it was exactly what he was thinking. She felt fire lick through her veins.

He sucked in his breath. "If you've got someone in the bedroom, tell him to leave," he ordered in a deceptively quiet tone. "We have unfinished business."

He'd seen Wayne's pickup and had jumped to conclusions. "T-there's no one here b-but me," she stammered enough to be heard, but the trembling of her limbs had taken over her ability to function with any coherence.

"I don't believe you." His voice grated. The next thing she knew, he swept past her to explore the rest of the trailer. He moved about the claustrophobic interior as if it were his divine right. *Because he didn't know any other way.*

Gaby wouldn't want him any other way. There was only one Luca Provere, and he was here in this trailer instead of in Rome. She didn't know what it meant, but she thought she might die of joy.

Like shockwaves, the tension suffused her being as he reentered the tiny living-room-cum-kitchen. "Why didn't you open the door to me?" His fierce demand caught her off guard.

Swallowing hard, she said, "B-because I couldn't believe it was you. Seven days ago you took final vows." Her voice shook. "I—I never expected to see you again. I thought maybe I was imagining you. You have to understand that I was afraid to open the door, for fear that y-you wouldn't be there after all," she admitted in a tremulous tone.

There was a brief pause while he studied her classic features, the passionate mold of her mouth. Then his questing eyes fell lower, over every line and curve of her quivering frame.

"Why did you run away from me in Lugano?"

She averted her eyes, twisting her hands together. "You know why," she whispered.

"Tell me!" he snapped.

"Because—" she began, "because I didn't trust myself to be around you."

"Why?"

He wasn't about to give up. He'd keep digging away until he had answers.

"Because you were a priest and I had no right to think of you as a man."

"If I hadn't been a priest, would you have opened your door to me that night?"

After a long silence she whispered, "Yes," and heard another sharp intake of breath.

"Have you ever made love with a man before?"

Her cheeks burned. "No."

"Then why me?" He was utterly relentless.

"Why are you torturing me like this?" she blurted in agony, looking everywhere except at him.

"Because I want to hear the words." He moved closer. "You just told me you've never let another man touch you. So why would you have let *me* make love to you?"

"The reason doesn't matter." By now he'd backed her up against the edge of the kitchen counter. "Now I really don't know why you've come, but—"

"The truth, Gabriella!" He sounded like a man who couldn't take any more.

She couldn't, either.

"Because I fell in love with you," she began in a husky voice. "Because I'll always be in love with you, and it hurts so much, I'm dying over it. There!" Her moist eyes darkened in intensity as she finally looked up at him. "You have my confession. Are you satisfied now, *Father Luca*?"

He grasped her shoulders, his black gaze impaling her. "That's not my name, so never use it again."

"W-what do you mean?"

His fingers tightened on her flesh through the soft material of her shirt. "To take final vows meant losing myself to the will of a higher authority. It meant never looking back at what might have been."

His palms molded to her shoulders possessively. "I searched my soul and found I couldn't make those sacred promises wholeheartedly. To stay would have been a lie... So I left." His voice dropped several registers.

Gaby stood there in shock. "But you've planned for this your entire life!" She simply couldn't comprehend what he was telling her. "What happened to change everything, to change you?"

His eyes smouldered. "*You're* what happened to me," he cried softly before his dark head descended, blotting out the light. "Help me, *mia testarossa*. Give me what I've been hungering for," he murmured feverishly before his mouth closed over hers with a savagery that told of his deep need.

She wanted answers to so many questions, but couldn't think of one. After the deprivation of the past month, to be in his arms like this without the accompanying guilt of knowing he was a priest turned her startled gasp into a moan of surrender.

Like a tenacious vine, Gaby wound her arms around his neck and embraced him with primitive longing, feasting on his mouth which had the power to drive her to mindless ecstasy. One kiss melted into another. What had been ignited in that cherry tree caused their hands and bodies to become an extension of each other.

"You're so beautiful, so *squisita*." He muttered thrilling endearments in his native tongue against her mouth and throat, his breathing as ragged as hers.

Rapture transported her. She had no idea how they happened to end up on the couch. The need to become one flesh was fast turning into a reality as Luke's body followed hers down against the cushions.

"I want you so much, Gabriella, I don't think I can wait," he admitted. His eyes glazed with raw desire before he buried his face in her fragrant hair. His accent had become more pronounced, underlining the depth of his passion.

Gaby feared this might be a dream and held him tighter. "Don't stop loving me, darling. Please—you're my whole life. Don't ever stop—" she begged, once more finding his mouth with her own, allowing him no escape.

Consumed by mutual wants, both were driven to assuage; neither of them heard footsteps outside. Not until the fury in her brother's voice penetrated her brain, did a cognizance of her surroundings come back to Gaby, particularly the door dangling from the only twisted hinge left holding it.

"You've got one second to get off my sister before I blow your head to kingdom come, you *animal*!"

"*No, Wayne! Don't shoot!*" Gaby screamed when she saw the barrel of the shotgun pointed at Luke's back.

In a lightning move, Luke had gotten to his feet, but Gaby was faster and leaped in front of him, protecting him with her own trembling body.

The confusion on her brother's face before he lowered the gun would have been funny if the situation hadn't been so precarious.

"I know what this looks like, Wayne, but you'd be completely wrong in anything you're assuming. This is the man I love!" Her throbbing voice rang with the undeniable declaration.

"I'm Luca Provere," the man behind her spoke up boldly before she could officially introduce them. With possessive hands that caressed her waist in response to her unequivocal pronouncement, he pulled her against his hard chest, letting her know he wanted her right there, that she wasn't to move.

"It's a privilege to meet you, Wayne. I've heard about you and your brothers. Please accept my apology for the damage done to the door. Naturally I'll have it repaired. Gabriella didn't believe that I had come for her."

He encircled her in his arms. "Drastic measures were needed to convince her otherwise," he drawled, nestling his chin in her hair.

A distinct blush covered her neck and face, causing her brother's mouth to twitch. Gaby saw admiration and respect for Luke in her brother's eyes. Wayne's approval meant a great deal.

"She's been waiting for you, Luke. It's been hell around here. I was about to apply a few drastic measures myself. What took you so long?"

She heard Luke's satisfied chuckle. "Gaby and I became acquainted in Italy, but because of extremely unusual and delicate circumstances, we parted on less than satisfactory terms. As soon as it was humanly possible, I came after her."

"Thank the Lord," Wayne murmured. "Under the circumstances, I apologize for interrupting. While you two finish getting reacquainted, I'll mosey down to the shed and get the tools I need to fix the door."

His blue eyes—identical to Gaby's—glanced at the splinters on the floor, then he winked at her. "Judging by the look of things, it'll take me a while to find everything I need."

When he left the trailer, Luke spun her around. "I like your brother very much," he whispered against her lips before devouring them all over again. "He has the good sense to know we need our privacy."

Gaby nodded wordlessly, too entranced by their physical proximity to think, let alone talk. She never wanted to be apart from him, not for one single second. Overflowing with the love she had to give him, she began raining kisses on his face, then captured his mouth.

But when he unexpectedly broke their kiss and put her firmly away from him, she groaned in agony, staring at him with wounded eyes.

His breathing grew shallow. "*Mio Dio*. Don't look at me like that," he grated. "You don't think I'm in as much pain as you are?" He raked his hands through his hair. "We have to talk, Gabriella, and talking is a physical impossibility when I feel your beautiful body melting into mine. It's best your brother broke in on us when he did."

With those words, the joy went out of her world. "Is that because you're going to leave me as soon as you tell me the reason for your unannounced visit? Are you trying to do the noble thing by saving me from myself?" Raw pain laced her questions. "If that's the case, I wish to heaven you'd never come!"

A spate of unintelligible Italian escaped his lips. "If I weren't in love with you, if I didn't place that love above duty, do you honestly believe I'd have broken down that door to get to you for any other reason?" His challenge resonated in the minuscule interior.

Her heart hammered unnaturally. "Y-you're in love with me?"

He expelled a tortured sigh. "*Sì, signorina*. The moment my little brother introduced us, my life was thrown into utter chaos, and that was something that has never happened to me before."

"Are you saying that you decided not to take your vows b-because of *me*?"

Lines darkened his face. "Sit down, Gabriella. This is going to take some time to explain and I can't do that when you are standing this close, looking so desirable that all I can think about is crushing you in my arms."

After hearing his admission, she was hardly able to breathe and did his bidding by subsiding on the couch where they'd lain so briefly. But she couldn't keep still.

"Please, before you tell me anything else, how is Giovanni? I care for him so much."

Luke took a deep breath. "Giovanni is in Assisi. He has begun his training to be a priest."

A priest. She mouthed the words.

They stared hard at each other for timeless moments while Gaby reflected on Giovanni whose spiritual makeup had separated him from the worldliness of men.

"I—I never expected to hear a revelation like that. Yet I can't honestly say I'm surprised."

"Nor can I," Luke concurred.

"The night of the accident, he inferred that it would be noble to die for a sacred love. But I thought—I thought he was discreetly warning me not to fall in love with you!"

"He's happy for the first time in his life. To think he fooled everyone all these years, Gabriella. He never told the family of his spiritual leanings, or his soul-changing experience at Assisi. Only you were privy to that information."

"But it makes perfect sense, Luke. He loved you so much, he didn't want to take anything away from you or your parents' dreams for you."

She rose to her feet, unable to stay seated. "Everything's becoming clear to me. On our drive to the *pensione* after dinner, he kept telling me how worried he was about you. He said you were such a noble person, you always put everyone else's needs ahead of your own. I finally asked him if he was upset that you wanted to serve the church."

Luke's black eyes pierced hers. "What did he tell you?"

"He said he wanted that for you more than anything in the world, but only if it was going to make you happy."

He rubbed the back of his neck. "My brother knew me better than I knew myself."

The mysterious tone of his voice prompted her to ask him what he meant.

"It's very simple. Giovanni knew I never had a vocation for the priesthood."

"*Never?*" she whispered. "You mean you went through all those years of training to please your parents?"

"Nothing is that simple, Gabriella. I grew up knowing nothing else and went along with it. I'll always be grateful for the excellent education I received, the great minds who imparted their knowledge. There were men I loved, men who will one day rise to become great men. I'm not sorry for the years I spent learning about God. It was all to my good.

"But to answer your question, I never received the calling. That's the reason I left Rome to go home and help Giovanni run the estate after our father died. I knew the most important ingredient for my life as a priest was missing. I thought that if I went back to the family, maybe my life would be touched in some way to let me know I should take final vows.

"Unfortunately, I received no special witness. On the other hand, my life at home held no particular attraction for me, either. There were several women, but the relationships were brief and unsatisfying. I felt like I was caught between two dimensions. Nothing was clear."

Gaby's eyes began to prickle with tears. "How awful for you."

His expression grew bleak. "I won't lie to you. For a time, I floundered. But in the end, I chose to serve the church because I knew it would be a good life and make my mother happy."

"Giovanni was right about everything," she murmured emotionally.

Luke nodded. "Over the years my brother observed all of this while keeping his own burning desire a secret. And then he met *you*. That's when he conceived his cunning plan."

The way he said it sent a chill chasing across her skin. "What plan?"

He shifted his weight. "When you fled from me in Lugano, I concluded that it was best not to go after you until I'd confronted Giovanni. To my surprise, he was at the palace waiting to confront me.

"We said a lot of things to each other. Things that should have been said years ago. During the course of that conversation he confessed that he knew I was unhappy, that he'd been praying to find a way to help me find peace in my life.

"He said that from the moment he met you, he had the unmistakable conviction that you and I were meant for each other. All it would take was for us to meet and spend time together."

She buried her face in her hands. "I don't believe what I'm hearing."

"Only Giovanni could have hatched such a plot, planning every move like he would a chess strategy. Even the accident was deliberate."

At that revelation, Gaby's eyes widened in shock. "But he could have been killed!"

"No, Gabriella. He staged everything to make it look that way. In reality, he influenced the doctor and staff to say he had a concussion so that you and I would be forced to stay together. Worse, he planted the jewelry, then arranged for the police to arrest you and lock you up so I'd have to come and bail you out. At that point, he knew I was so in love with you, I'd never return to Rome."

Her throat constricted. "He loved you enough to do all that?"

"He loves you, too," Luke said in a haunting whisper. "All that's left to make his joy complete is to hear that you have agreed to become my wife."

He moved swiftly, cupping her flushed face in his hands. "You have to marry me, Gabriella." His voice shook. "I knew I wanted you for myself long before the dinner at the palace concluded. That's why I left the table when I did, because I suddenly discovered that the missing ingredient in my life had been sitting at my side all evening, torturing me with invitation, and my hands were tied for more than one reason."

Gaby moaned. "I couldn't bear it when you got up and left so quickly. I was afraid I'd never see you again. It was one of the worst moments of my life. Much as I hated to learn that Giovanni had been in an accident, I was overjoyed when you came to the *pensione* for me."

Luke brushed her lips with his own. "He didn't have to manufacture a reason for me to stay in Urbino. Nothing could have made me return to Rome. I was determined to spend the next day with you."

Her eyes glowed a hot blue. "It was a time I'll never forget. That's when I knew I'd fallen so deeply in love with you, I realized that if I couldn't be your wife, I'd probably remain single because no other man could ever compare to you."

She slid her hands up his warm chest, feeling the heavy thud of his heart. "I adore you, my darling Luca. There's nothing more I could ask of life than to be your wife, but I'm afraid your mother won't approve."

Luke felt the contour of her lips with his thumb. "Mother surprised both Giovanni and me by giving us her blessing. After the three of us sat down together, she, too, had some confessions to make. Among them, the fact that she'd sensed for some time that neither of us was truly happy.

"She insisted that it was her fault for thrusting something on me which should have been my choice. She also blames herself for not seeing Giovanni's pain. At this point, Mother is so over-joyed that one of us is going to get married and provide her with grandchildren, she's ready to give you a proper welcome. As for the rest of the family, you won them over at dinner."

"Thank you for telling me that," was all Gaby could manage to say in her emotion-filled state.

His expression sobered. "I have yet to meet your parents. How are they going to feel about their only daughter living in Italy?"

"They won't be at all surprised. The whole family knows I fell painfully in love while I was abroad. Daddy half expected it because of my great-grandmother's history, but no one knows the details. I couldn't bring myself to talk about it, not when I thought you were lost to me forever."

The memory of so much unhappiness made her shudder and she clung to him all the harder.

"We'll leave for Las Vegas now. I want to marry you as soon as we can, surrounded by your family and friends. Later we'll renew our vows in Assisi with my family in attendance."

She smiled up at him, blinding him with its radiance. "I can't wait to be Signora Luca Francesco della Provere."

He lowered his head and smothered her with kisses. "I can't wait to give you one of your wedding presents."

"You already have presents for me?"

"Let's just say that this one has been sitting in Tivoli for years, waiting to be discovered."

Her mind began turning over all the possibilities. Tivoli was an ancient city outside Rome. "Does this have something to do with my great-grandmother?" she cried in pure delight.

A mysterious smile broke out on his handsome face. "You're going to have to wait for the truth until we've taken our vows *mia testarossa*."

She sucked in her breath. "I feel like I already made mine in that cherry tree."

"We both did," he murmured thickly. "But humor me once more, Gabriella." His black eyes burned with an intensity of feeling. "I need legal permission to love you so I can really start to live..."

EPILOGUE

LUKE'S mother, resplendent in tearose pink *peau de soie*, rang the small crystal bell, signaling that she wanted the attention of everyone in the wedding party.

Throughout the succulent feast served immediately after the five o'clock ceremony in the palace chapel, Gaby had been aware of Luke's possessive hand on her thigh beneath the dining room table.

A month ago he'd followed her to Nevada. She didn't know how they'd survived the marriage preparations this long without going to bed together. But they'd both agreed that waiting until their wedding night to make love for the first time would be their priceless gift to each other.

Too feverish to do anything more than toy with her food, she slid her hand over his, aware that in just a little while, her new husband would become her lifetime lover. Unable to do otherwise, she lifted adoring blue eyes to him. The devouring look in his thrilled her almost to the consuming of her flesh.

He lifted her hand and kissed the palm. "It's time we forgot the world and concentrated on each other."

"Darling—" she whispered breathlessly at the husky tone of his deep voice, "I still can't believe I'm your wife. The last time we sat at this table, yo—"

"Don't think about it, Gabriella. That is all in the past, when I was a different man."

She clung to his hand. "I—I hope your mother will come to accept me one day."

"Mama is making great strides. By the time we produce a new little Provere, she'll be calling you her treasured daughter." Gaby blushed. "If you'll notice, the portrait of my illustrious ancestor no longer dominates this room."

"I hadn't realized!" she blurted. Being with Luke caused the world around her to recede because *he* was her world. She loved him with a fierceness that almost frightened her.

"One day soon a painting of Giovanni will grace that wall."

Just then Giovanni's warm brown eyes captured her attention from across the table and they both smiled. His face glowed with an inner happiness he no longer had to hide.

"If I don't miss my guess," Luke murmured, "Efresina is going to make a full recovery. Have you noticed how she and Ted haven't spent one minute apart since they met?"

"*Ted*?"

Shocked by Luke's observation, she gazed down the long table at her family. Everyone loved Luke and had come for the wedding. But they were overwhelmed to discover the kind of family she'd married into and were still looking a little dazed.

Ted, the shiest of her brothers, was not only dazed but smitten with the lovely Efresina. Her dark eyes sparkled from all the attention he was giving her.

Gaby darted her husband an illuminating smile. "Ted got his sandy-red hair from our great-grandmother. Something tells me we might be seeing a lot of him in the months to come."

His smile faded to be replaced by a look of such smoldering sensuality, her heart turned over. "As happy as I am for Efresina and your brother, I'm glad you said months, *mia testarossa*, because it's going to take that long before I'm willing to share you with anyone."

"Luca, we're all waiting to hear you say a few words," Giovanni prodded with an infectious grin.

In a swift movement, Luke rose to his feet and brought Gaby with him. Hugging her around the waist, he started toward the door. "I'm sorry, *fratello*," he called over his shoulder, "but Gabriella and I need to do some communicating of our own first."

With her heart thudding because she was finally going to get her heart's desire, Gaby honored American custom and threw her bouquet over her head so it practically landed in Efresina's lap.

While everyone in the room responded with cries of excitement and laughter, her husband exercised his age-old right as Duke of Urbino and carried off the most willing, besotted maiden in the Marches to the bridal chamber.

New York Times **Bestselling Author**

REBECCA BRANDEWYNE

FOR GOOD OR FOR EVIL— THE INSIDE STORY...

The noble Hampton family, with its legacy of sin and scandal, suffers the ultimate tragedy: the ruthless murder of one of its own.

There are only two people who can unravel the case—

JAKE SERINGO is the cynical cop who grew up on the mean streets of life;

CLAIRE CONNELLY is the beautiful but aloof broadcast journalist.

They'd parted years ago on explosive terms—now they are on the trail of a bizarre and shocking family secret that could topple a dynasty.

GLORY SEEKERS

The search begins at your favorite retail outlet in June 1997.

MIRA **The brightest star in women's fiction**

Look us up on-line at: http://www.romance.net

MRBGS

And the Winner Is...
You!

...when you pick up these great titles
from our new promotion at your
favorite retail outlet this June!

Diana Palmer
The Case of the Mesmerizing Boss

Betty Neels
The Convenient Wife

Annette Broadrick
Irresistible

Emma Darcy
A Wedding to Remember

Rachel Lee
Lost Warriors

Marie Ferrarella
Father Goose

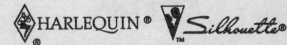

Look us up on-line at: http://www.romance.net   ATWI397-R

HARLEQUIN ULTIMATE GUIDES™

GLIDE THROUGH ANY EVENT WITH THE LATEST ETIQUETTE EXPERTISE!

A stuffy etiquette book? Absolutely not! This is an up-to-date, lighthearted approach to etiquette, aimed at getting you through the many occasions and special events you'll be called on to attend or host.

- trade secrets of overnight visitors who actually get invited back
- inside tips for every bride, groom and wedding attendee
- how to gracefully exit a boring conversation
- how to handle the boss's birthday
- how to be the perfect guest or host

Everything you need to ensure that you're always

RISING
TO THE
OCCASION

Available in July at your favorite Harlequin retail outlet.

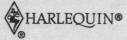
HARLEQUIN®

Look us up on-line at: http://www.romance.net   RISING

HE SAID

♥

SHE SAID

Explore the mystery of male/female communication in this extraordinary new book from two of your favorite Harlequin authors.

Jasmine Cresswell and Margaret St. George bring you the exciting story of two romantic adversaries—each from their own point of view!

DEV'S STORY. CATHY'S STORY.
As he sees it. As she sees it.
Both sides of the story!

The heat is definitely on, and these two can't stay out of the kitchen!

Don't miss **HE SAID, SHE SAID.**
Available in July wherever Harlequin books are sold.

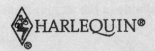 HARLEQUIN®

Look us up on-line at: http://www.romance.net   HESAID

He changes diapers, mixes formula and
tells wonderful bedtime stories—he's

Three totally different stories of sexy, single
heroes each raising another man's child...
from three of your favorite authors:

MEMORIES OF THE PAST
by Carole Mortimer

THE MARRIAGE TICKET
by Sharon Brondos

TELL ME A STORY
by Dallas Schulze

Available this June wherever
Harlequin and Silhouette books are sold.

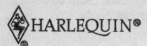 HARLEQUIN®  Silhouette®

Look us up on-line at: http://www.romance.net   HREQ697

TAYLOR SMITH

Who would you trust with your life?
Think again.

A tranquil New England town is rocked to its core when a young coed is linked to a devastating crime—then goes missing.

One woman, who believes in the girl's innocence, is determined to find her before she's silenced...forever. Her only ally is a man who no longer believes in anyone's innocence. But is he an ally?

At a time when all loyalties are suspect, and old friends may be foes, she has to decide—quickly—who can be trusted. The wrong choice could be fatal.

The Best of Enemies

Available at your favorite retail outlet in June 1997.

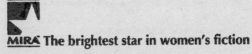

MIRA The brightest star in women's fiction

Look us up on-line at: http://www.romance.net

MTSTBE